The Jellyfish Generation

By

Mary Wirth Fenner

CeShore

Pittsburgh, PA

ISBN 1-58501-026-X

Trade Paperback

First Printing — 2001
Library of Congress #00-109269

Request for information should be addressed to:

CeShore Publishing Company
The Sterling Building
440 Friday Road
Pittsburgh, PA 15209
www.ceshore.com

CeShore is an imprint of SterlingHouse Publisher, Inc.
Cover Design: Michelle S. Lenkner — SterlingHouse Publisher, Inc.
Book Design: Kathleen M. Gall
Ink sketches by Mary Wirth Fenner
Cover photographs provided by Mary Wirth Fenner

Printed in the United States of America

For Jack V., Jack N., Anne M.,
with all my love and admiration.

Sincere and special thanks
to my family and to friends for
their erudite proofreading
and/or kind encouragement.
Ruth Ann Bender, Stuart Bender, Phil Carleton,
Jack N. Fenner, Jack V. Fenner,
Judy Helvey, Ian Henderson, Rita Henderson,
Anne M. Jensen, Carolyn Malone,
Phyl Moore, Sylvia Patchin, Ruth Smith,
Kathy VanderBroek, Ken VanderBroek, Dick Votaw.
Green River Writer's Group:
Sara Hoskinson Frommer, Bob Weir, Mary Harrison,
"Mac" McDaniel.

A little house well fill'd,
a little field well till'd,
and a little wife well will'd
are great riches.

—Poor Richard's Almanack

"No! Not 'Henri'! What about Christmas cards!" I spluttered.

Over thirty years ago I said those ridiculous words and I even tacked on, "No hilarious name shall fall upon the next generation!" for emphasis. That outburst is seared into my memory like the motto on the wooden plaque given me by Helen, my poetess: "No poem was ever written by a drinker of water." But, you see, the occasion was our son's birth, and I was nervous.

Our son's downy head lay against my wife's bulging chest, the air was heavy with sweet baby lotion, and I was just a person who had entered from the wings on the cue, "You have a boy." I hadn't helped her breathe or anything: a disgrace to my sex. We had agreed on that. I mean, that I would not come into her room to help her breathe or anything. She knew five years before, I realize, before I even knew that we'd be making a down payment on a house instead of a boat-'n-motor, she knew that the kind of man who could gut a fish and cut his thumb and drive himself to the ER and then keel over when he held his hand out to the doctor, she knew then that she would not care to be jarred by my head hitting her bed and/or delivery table. So, dressed in a blue gown and feeling myself being influenced by the purity pervading the room, I was moved to add some leveling effect to my previous splutter: "I know it's only June, Helly. But it's bad enough getting cards signed 'Judy, Jane, Jerome, and Ginny Johnsten' as if they were stuck in Alliteration Alley with both exits blocked. What if we had *more* children! No, no, not for years. But even if we don't, you wouldn't be able to resist: Happy Holidays from Henry, Helen, Henrietta, and Henri Hilarious." Mother and son remained calm. In fact, Helen revealed the slightest twinkle to me, the first I'd seen in over six months, so I was encouraged to continue. I said, "If I had kept my name while all about me were changing theirs, you'd be Hilarious, my son." That brought a tired wifey smile.

Gathering up the warm blue bundle of boy into my arms and looking into his big eyes looking back at me so seriously and, it seemed, quizzically, I bent my head and whispered, "Son, the truth is that your name might truly have been Hilarious. You see, my Grandpa had pronounced his name as clearly as he could in his rolling, guttural German—which at any rate was clearer than his flourishy script. He said, 'Herr Albert Virt' which the immigration officer heard as 'Hairarralveers', wrote as 'Herrlarious', and said, 'Okay, Mr. Hilarious, standen der.' Grandpa didn't care what the official wrote down as long as he could go stand on the accepted side, the America Side. He came to Michigan and married a German-born lady, and they had eleven children with German-sounding names like Gustave and Frieda. Trying to become truly Americans, they named their twelfth child 'Kind' which looked kind in English but was pronounced 'kint' in German. That child, Kind Hilarious, grew up and named his first-born son 'Kind' who was referred to as 'das kleine Kind.' That was me: your daddy. And I was 'Kind' for 21 years until I put an end to the silly name business. I paid a clerk $10 and became Henry K. (for Kind) Virtson, grandson of Herr Virt himself. Your mother, however, still thinks I'm sometimes hilarious and keeps the family joke alive at odd times such as when signing Christmas cards. So you see, son, we always have to keep The Reasonable Man with us. He and I fended off 'Henrietta,' which your sister Elizabeth would have been blessed with had we not been on watch and moved it to the middle. But you've closed your eyes, and, I see, so has your mommy."

I handed my blue bundle of boy over to someone who appeared wearing a yellow smock and a big smile and who in return gave me another paper requesting the child's name. In the blank was Helen's printing: *Jack*? I crossed off the question mark, filled in the rest, and smiled. "I shoulda known," I said to Helen's peaceful albeit smug face. "You just wanted to hear my bedtime story again!"

At home I paid the sitter and went into Elizabeth's bedroom. I whispered to her—angelic sleeping child—that her baby brother arrived, that he's one year and 50 weeks younger than she is and that she shouldn't be jealous of the time her mommy would spend with him. But being the sweetest of the sweet, she would love him, I knew, and lead the way for him in the world. Helen would have Elizabeth's devoted "help" while I would be off earning a living and not thinking at all about what was happening with the children until I returned home at the end of the day. After I brushed her curly, damp hair off her forehead with my cheek, I went to get a beer, settled in my chair, and flipped up the footrest.

The years were getting very busy, at least when compared with the easy flow of a weekly date, for instance. Helen and I spent three years adhering to the well-known though unspoken dating rituals of the 1950s, ruled mainly by the "reasonable man"—one married only when all else failed. But finally, it was Helen's "reasonable woman" who convinced me that marriage would be a most desirable tender trap, since all else had failed and would continue to fail until we were married. We had met on a blind date arranged by a mutual friend in the spring of '54. I was one of 400 new employees who flooded into the little city of 15,000 in mid-Michigan in 1953. Most of us who were bachelors had already had our stint in the service, and we were ready to have fun hunting, fishing, golfing, dating, and working for a fledgling company that had a bright future. Helen came to town as a teacher, the first without previous teaching experience as the schools rushed to handle the influx of new students. The city was declared "dry" many years ago, but there was a nice eatery, bar, and dance floor just outside the city limits. That's where we went on that first blind date. We met my two roommates and their dates and we all danced with each other's partner and had a good time. Helen confessed much later that seeing three mature men all over 6'2" was so wonderful that she would have have married any of us three. She's 5'8".

When the tiny silver smelt began their springtime runs, we took our nets and went dipping in the river at midnight. We went to movies at the only theater in town. (Its sound kicked out at least once during every film.) We did a bit of skiing, golfing, dancing, and laughing, and when Helen (slyly, I later learned) announced that she and her roommate had decided to "try teaching in another state next year," I agreed to be caught, at which point we gave to each other all of our love, loyalty, friendship and fun. And now, with the birth of our boy, we knew the wheel of time just got a quick spin, a spin way beyond the attitudes and behaviors we had been accustomed to.

I'm sitting in the same spot—new chair, though—37 years after our son's birth. Helen is sitting near the large windows that overlook the back yard and a small football field-sized neighborhood park. We had contributed the huge sum of $50 back in 1959 for the privilege of bordering it and furnishing it with a swing set and a sandbox. Now the view is invaluable. Helen's chair is of Scandinavian design. She says she needs the uprightness for her needlework projects; whereas I need the lazy style for, ah, thinking. The ottoman at her feet is her acquiescence to repose. She's ten feet to my left, doing her needlepoint or knitting or crocheting or whichever it is tonight. All eventually make something wonderful out of the initial long string of nothing. She likes that chair and I like mine. We moved mine over there once, hers over here because I was cold and wore a sweat shirt but sat by the door; Helen was always too warm and sat in the airless corner. It's ridiculous, but I didn't like the change. It's the same at the kitchen table. We sit on the same chairs we sat on when it was necessary for each of us to be next to a child and I had to be able to look out the window for my car pool to arrive back in the days when we had only one car and Helen got to use it twice a week. She once mused aloud about the irony of those days: "Life is backwards. When I was totally rushed for time, we had one car, no frost-free refrigerator, no self-clean oven, no no-wax floor, no freezer, no microwave and now we have all those things and don't really need them."

I said, "We had a dishwasher but you never used it."

She said, "That was because we didn't have enough dishes to get through the day and I had to wash my non-safe pots and pans by hand anyway."

I said, "You still don't use it."

She said, "I always used to use it when we had company. Now, of course, we don't dirty enough dishes in three days and I still have to wash my non-safe pots and pans by hand anyway."

"Well," I said, amicably, "we were young and didn't even notice what we didn't have."

She said, "But it would have been wonderful to have had everything reversed. Except for the one-car bit. Wouldn't you go crazy hearing my 'I need the car, dear' every three hours?"

And I said, "I'd go crazy to hear you call me 'dear' every three hours," and our banter faded away as it always does, with no conclusion necessary. So we sit ten feet apart and every night we share the newspaper and throw the section we've finished: good shot, or, oops.

There's a comfortable new couch between us but she never uses it unless she is recovering from something, and I only use it when I can't sleep and haul my book, a pillow, and an afghan out here at 4 a.m. while Helen snores away. The papers, therefore, have to clear the interference of the couch. Helen sometimes says that this throwing business reminds her of one of the funniest segments in *Bleak House* by Dickens. When she told me what it was about, I decided not to read the book even if it did shame lawyers in England and we could use the same shame in this country. As she tells it, this very old husband and wife sit side by side in comfy chairs at their daughter's house. They are feeble. Of course, there's no TV, no radio, and they cannot see well enough to read. They do not speak to each other. The daughter tends to their needs. The wife has a long grudge against the husband: he lost their money. The husband's grudge against the wife is her nagging. But about once a day, she asks her husband what time it is. He replies with something that sounds to her like "tuppence," and, remembering their lost savings, this reference to money causes her such renewed anger that her energy returns long enough for her to grab the pillow from her chair, reach over, and pound her husband with it while hollering "tuppence! tuppence!" He is helplessly pummeled down, down into his clothes until his daughter comes and fluffs him up again.

It sure doesn't sound funny to me. Nobody else has ever referred to *Bleak House* as having one drop of humor in it. But Helen sure does seem to enjoy throwing the paper at me, to me.

Sometimes she walks over to my chair and places a sheet of yellow, lined paper on my end table. A poem is written on it, a poem she composed and wants my layman's opinion about before entrusting it to the cold eye of a contest judge. She insists that I don't have to "know poetry" to do this favor, that poetry is an emotional thing (hence the drinker-of-water plaque) and that all I have to do is follow the punctuation. She doesn't write much free verse which, she warmly proclaims, Robert Frost said is "like playing tennis without a net." When learning tennis, Helen played often without a net but would never, ever play without one now. "Most free verse poets are still at the netless level," she quips. Anyway, my critiquing consists of choosing one word out of my list of about four in my vocabulary that would qualify for judging poetry and writing it in pencil at the top of the page. That evidently tells her tons of necessary information because she invariably takes the page to the kitchen table and writes and is still writing when I turn off the bedroom light. Her most recent offering is a poem called "Loving." I understand it. I like it. I'll probably write "Nice"at the top. This one is about us. I think. Helen does have a profound imagination. It's certainly about *her*, if not me. Yet, I've never figured out if I'm supposed to get a hint of what kind of mood she might be in by reading what she's written. If I am, what does this one mean?

Like a waiting spark explodes
into a blaze of hands
that reach to wrap a pine in bands
of fire—like that, your love explodes
upon my heart; your eagerness erodes
my timid soul by its commands
to love you. But my love demands
some gentleness, romantic odes
with a knight-and-maiden sound.
So bring me daisies or a rose; persist
with silly nothings, make me smile,
but don't let love be quick nor too profound.
Let it waken like a baby, kissed
so sweetly that it stirs, yet sleeps awhile.

Well, since she likes my reading them and writing my one word, I do.

Not that I read all the stuff she writes and reads. Her tastes in reading are wider than mine, probably because I like to be entertained and then incidentally informed whereas she likes to be informed and incidentally entertained. But we both like Disney's awesome portrayal of pure, sweet, unadulterated, mind-boggling innocence when Bambi is learning to identify things. He noses a skunk in a patch of flowers and asks "flower?" which sends Thumper into rolling fits of laughter, but "Flower" the skunk is shyly pleased. Afraid she could not bear to see Bambi crying "Mother? Mother?" she avoided seeing the movie again, but one night our grandchildren brought the newly-released tape and insisted. Jack brought her a stiff drink. She watched. Nothing happened to her emotions except relief that Gordie and Ben did not get upset over the motherless Bambi but were more concerned about the ferocious dogs; however, she already knew the ending so could reassure them that Bambi would survive. She laughed at Bambi's sliding on the ice—my favorite part—and she realized that she had indeed grown up. Such depths to motherhood and grandmahood! That was one hobgoblin vanquished.

Hobgoblin: I haven't thought of that word in quite a few years. Who was that teacher, what the heck was her name, can't remember anything anymore … it was the sixth grade, way before the Blur Years of the 1960s when Helen's brother-in-law enriched our lives and the hippies and assassinations and all-around bedlam made us wonder if we had been transported to some evil ship and shoved down a gangplank to some other country where there was no Reasonable Man and nobody ever heard of Common Sense, much less plain decency. It must have been 1940: a good time, for kids.

A guy like me would scuff through school doing the best he could to avoid embarrassing anybody. It was Mrs. Char, short for Charjewakowski, I think, who made our hobgoblin so notorious. She loved the Sayings in *Poor Richard's Almanack* that Franklin compiled between his printing and his improving every area of the lives of his fellow citizens. She had many occasions in our class that called forth from her a Saying. If a student marked up his desk with, say, an outline of a football or initials or deep grooves resembling railroad tracks to nowhere, she'd tell him sternly, "Doors and walls are fool's papers" and then he'd have to recite that while sanding off the marks that included those made by earlier generations of kids. She also liked to quote Sayings that were funnily informative: Fish and visitors stink after three days. Once she assigned homework that was only one line long: write a modern saying, one that could be applied today. Well, we boys were happy to count on knocking that off and having free time for pickup basketball in our driveway. We played ball, but the next day only one guy out of the whole class including the usually conscientious girls had done the homework.

Mrs. Char wrote his proffered saying on the board: All generalizations are false including this one. "Brilliant," I thought, "and it'll take her mind off the rest of us who haven't written anything." Then she asked if he had help writing it. He said his Dad helped. And, she said, Mark Twain and Alexander Dumas helped him. Then to our relief she just went on to discuss the difficulties of coining precise wisdom that would last across generations. She tossed out "Three can keep a secret if two of them are dead." We laughed like heck and looked at the giggling girls who seemed to sense it was quite true. She wrote several more sayings on the blackboard and we all copied them:

1. God works wonders now and then; behold! a lawyer, an honest man.
2. Love, a cough, and a smoke can't well be hid.
3. Men and melons are hard to know.
4. A house without a woman and firelight is like a body without soul or spirit.

There was no equivalent in the Almanack for Not in my backyard, In your face, Get a life, Sue me.

I wonder if old Mrs. Char knew that the world was moving faster and that she had better provide us kids with something to hang onto. Is that why she returns to me so clearly now, now that I am the old age she was when she was teaching? I can see her writing on the dusty board with her upper arms slightly flapping under her long-sleeved, silky, blue blouse that tied in a perfect bow under her collar bones, and turning to peer at us who had snorted at the name "Rudyard" and had whispered "Must be someone who's dead." But we learned "If." I even learned some of the lines—

If you can bear to hear the truth you've spoken
Twisted by knaves to make a trap for fools
Or watch the things you gave your life to, broken
And stoop and build 'em up with worn-out tools …

and finally, if you could do a whole bunch of noble things, then you'd be a MAN. Whew. That was a big order. I particularly didn't like rebuilding things with worn-out tools, but I got the drift of the thing, and so did the girls who perhaps unknowingly held to that wonderful ideal as their idea of a MAN, one who would someday be a husband. He would be out there somewhere waiting for the right girl. It was wonderful optimism, wonderful guide to a goal. Why not? Something has to pull people forward, be inspiring.

Besides Kipling, there was that one-man show, that master of the one-liners, that first American philosopher to stress the good American self-reliance and sincerity and hard-working individualism that pulled us away from European dominance in our way of life. Enter Ralph Waldo Emerson. His essays had to be studied one declarative sentence at a time, so the entire essay could take a week of classes just to dissect it. He said, for one thing, that "A foolish consistency is the hobgoblin of little minds." And Mrs. Char thought that was one of his better declaratives. When she cast about our class for a volunteer to explain it, I slunk down a bit and lowered my eyes. Sure as shootin' she called on me.

"What's a hobgoblin?" I parried.

"Look it up," she thrust. (Pause. Riffled pages.)

"It's not in the dictionary," I said, raising my visor.

"Tell us tomorrow," she said, putting her rapier on her desk.

The next day I triumphantly reported that a hobgoblin was a superstition. "So what does the line mean then?" she gently asked. Grind, grind. With contributions from eight or nine brighter kids, we worked something out that met with her approval: A person who does a foolish thing over and over because he's afraid to change will never amount to anything. Will never amount to anything! We knew absolutely what that meant. The local drunk never amounted to anything. He always looked sad, afraid, lonely. Each of us wanted, above all else, to amount to something.

Butterfly Words

(A tribute to Grandfather)

Now from the pinnacle of manhood
I can see its pyramidal base: I see no tonnage of stone

just orange seeds in a perfect row
put there with care and playful show.
There I see ten Indian pennies, each warrior a chief,
and the silver lucky piece, shining from intense belief.
I see a row of blocks towering to my chin—
exquisitely precarious, but "might one more block win?"
Here I see wide blades of grass to blow a foreign sound—
another good excuse to sit upon the ground.
But there, the stack of books! I hear again
butterfly-words soar from their printed cocoons …

I see all clearly now.
Through the snows of childhood doubt,
Past sanding sorrow, he led me
To where confidence began,
Molding within me
His criteria for a Man.

Over the years, Helen and I have slain several hobgoblins. We probably should have thanked Mrs. Char like Durante thanked Mrs. Callabash all those years. I hope Mrs. Char got a hint from us, though, that we'd amount to something. Come to think of it, she retired in '41, making our class her last. She was always smiling when we'd meet her at the butcher shop, so she must have felt she had done the right thing at the right time. She certainly had enough Sayings and Declaratives to guide her!

I wonder if we've finished with the hobgoblin business. You'd think after all this time we've earned the right to lower our defenses and go lean against the tractor at our berry acreage, chew on the juicy end of a long, grassy weed, and talk weather with the other retirees who come by to say "How ya doing?" and to get first-hand info on the last trip we took in case they would want to go there too. After the challenge of Jube, it seems to me we ought to have a long reprieve coming. Melons and men are hard to know, but at least you can thump a melon.

Jube and the Blur Years are inextricably fused, beginning when Elizabeth was about six and Jack, four. Before that their babyhood and toddler years were summed up as "sweet little girl" and "fine young boy" and "frantically busy Mommy" and "hard-working Daddy." I was a chemist, amounting to something by mixing up great stuff with endless possibilities for the company, and Helen was meanwhile making profound decisions every day that would shape our kids' futures, wanting only to be able to sit down and finish a cup of coffee. I found I had to pare down some of my activities that had hung over from my bachelor days. When my legs felt like cooked noodles, I stopped playing basketball. I turned down long fishing trips, hunted only once a year, and became a helpful father although neither one of us realized we were probably making sacrifices. We just adjusted our outside lives to our inside lives: family. Before we could take stock of where we were headed, the babies became a little girl and a little boy. And they loved Jube.

Good ol' funny, mustachioed Jube: he made all of us laugh. He had a mustache that went straight across until it reached a dimple and then it went sort of up and ended in the dimple crease. The kids broke their sides stifling laughs just watching him talk—the hairy ends of the stache seemingly waving at them like the black wands of a woolly caterpillar. What with a distinguishing feature like that, you'd think he was dashing, debonair, suave; but he was ex-Navy, a bit stocky although tall, wore uninteresting suits with dull ties and colored shirts, and looked more at ease in his old leather jacket with its innumerable deep pockets and his heavy gabardine pants. An outdoor guy, he liked fishing, crawling over rocks in faraway places on his many solo trips to who knew where. But his hands were clean; literally, that is. Figuratively, we learned later, they were a bit smudged from his connections with old ships and mysterious destinations. But to look at his hands, you'd figure he took more pride in their appearance than in the exact trim of his mustache. His visits always started with the same invitation from Helen:

"Why don't you come on over for Thanksgiving?"

Jube: It's a ten-hour drive. Probably on ice. Or in fog.

"But you don't have to bundle up any kids. And Hannah and I haven't gabbed for ages."

Jube: Well, we gotta find a place for Mynah and he always is half crazed with anxiety when we get him back from that pet shop.

"The kids are really looking forward to your visit."

Jube: I'll talk to Hannah.

Three days later, Hannah says, "Jube has something going, but if he gets back, we can make it the day after Thanksgiving, if that's okay?"

Helen is delighted. "Fine! Then we can go hit the stores while the turkey's baking. You'll love all the Christmas stuff at the Corner Crafts this year. Their Open House is that weekend."

Three days later, Jube asks, "Do you want us to bring some summer sausage? I've got a couple bottles of Late Times in the trunk already. Sure that's enough?"

So it was set. Helen began the swirling dervish routine of cleaning, grocery shopping, pie-baking and all the happy chores that go into having real adults coming for a visit, especially her own sister Hannah. The kids caught the excitement and jumped around yelling "Jubilant's coming! Jubilant's coming!" while organizing their rooms, making and putting up Christmas chains—too early but we didn't care—and conjuring up games with the small-car collection that involved turning the cars into people and having them go on long, involved trips. I'm not sure how that went, but it kept them occupied. Meanwhile I just went to work, happy that my wife and children were happy. Strange how we anticipated those happy visits just because grownups broke up our routine of planning events for the kids' enjoyment. And these visits were from relatives, yet! People who loved us as we did them.

Hannah jumped out of the Olds, her black hair upswept with no curl out of place, her lipstick renewed, her clothes uncrushed. Helen whispered, "Do they stop at the end of our block and beautify themselves?" Then Jube crawled out from behind the steering wheel with his hands still cramped into a grasp and walked outrageously bent over and moaned, "Why do you have to live so far away! I can't move!"

I asked, "Did you take a couple breaks?"

Jube replied, as usual, "Just one hurry-up pit stop. We brought coffee and oatmeal cookies along. Oh my achin' back." He groped his way to the kitchen, fixed himself a drink, straightened up, and then, looking at Elizabeth and Jack who had followed his nonsense with great glee, he suddenly said, "Well! If it isn't the Katzenjammer Kids! Here's something for you two to keep you out of my way," he teased, handing each a package. Jack's was a full Indian headdress. He was ecstatic. Jube explained, "Those are genuine imitation turkey feathers." Jack glowed. Over our trip-talks, I could hear Elizabeth's indignant "They aren't real, stupid!" and Jack's retort, "He said they are!" and Elizabeth's rebuttal, "Imitation means fake, stupid!" and Jack's defensive "What do *you* know, stupid!"

Meanwhile Jube began plumbing the depths of his assortment of facts as we hashed over the business of sports, the crookedness of politics, the rudeness and lack of training of store clerks, the latest gimmicks on cars, etc. When I thought we'd about covered everything, the sounds of voices grew fainter, and I was just about to tumble into blessed peace when Jube got up, refilled his dry manhattan and came back with another exclamation. "Geez! That ice at Benton Harbor really gets to me. Is there a salt shortage in this state? They shoulda been out there before we even left Wisconsin. I'd take those damn ferries if they weren't run by the railroads. If we *ever* have a decent, sunny drive over here ..." and then he was reminded of other icy and/or foggy and/or snowy trips here at Christmas, and of the one time at Easter when he built a big snow rabbit in our back yard. So he decided it was time to sing. Sooner or later, they always sang. They gathered around the piano, Helen played, and they sang their hearts out while I listened. Helen and Hannah remembered again their mother's singing while she accompanied herself on her baby grand piano downstairs. They'd be just about asleep in their shared room, and their older brother Nick would have just turned off his light in his room down the hall, when the eerie, high pitch of their mother's strong and full-bodied rendition of the Nelson Eddy and Jeanette Mac Donald favorite would waft up to their rooms: "When I'm calling you-u-u-ooo-ooo-ooo-

ooo,ooo,ooo, will you answer too-ooo-ooo-ooo-ooo,ooo,ooo," or, they wondered, was it "true-ue-ooo-ooo-ooo-ooo,ooo,ooo." Now they tried to imitate the sound but ended up laughing too hard amid Jube's comment, "Who let the coyotes in here?" Tone deaf as I am, I like music, and can even critique it, but I can't sing it. When I heard Jube's deep rendition of "Ol' Man River," I knew they were done and they'd have teary eyes of nostalgia.

The next morning, Jube, Jack and I went out to the woods to chop some wood, anticipating a fine fire after our huge dinner and maybe even a leftover college game. Hannah and Helen and Elizabeth hit the stores doing their "girl stuff," and we all returned to the aroma that filled the house: 22 lbs. of turkey needing to be basted; the oven actually dripped juice down its side as it huffed away on its big, important job. Ah, the anticipation!

While Jube and I settled into our chairs and Helen praised Jack for not getting in our ax's way and for not suffering untold wounds, we started a continuation of last night's discussions, albeit a lot slower and with significant pauses between topics. Helen and Hannah rushed around banging pots and kettles in the last hour of dinner preparations. All the side dishes had to be prepared on the stove burners—no room in the oven—and all were critical and legendary, especially the potato dumplings with the croutons stuffed in the centers. We eagerly came to the table at our first summons; Jube lifted a big drumstick with two hands because it "was so heavy" and plopped it on Jack's plate—Jack had expected it and smiled with the anticipation of actually finishing it off this time. We spent the next hour eating, talking, laughing. It was a celebration indeed.

We menfolk settled into our chairs again; Helen and Hannah banged in the kitchen again, filling the dishwasher and still having 45 minutes of washing, wiping, cleaning up, and jabbering in their happy sisterly way. Splinters of words flew from the kitchen—kni yar lefthan craz!—sailing over the heads of Elizabeth and Jack and landing on Jube's slumped form which prompted an exaggerated burp that made the kids look up at him, their cars in their hands in the air. He laughed and said, "Did you know piglets go to teats in the order in which they were born?" I said "Huh?" which really meant "What caused *that* association?" but he always had some mind-wandering type of comment after being warmed by food and friendship.

Helen would have been the better straight man because she's used to being put to the test by Nick; he calls periodically from Alaska and runs up his bill with oddball questions he knows she'll eventually find an answer to. Once it was "What's a Nittany lion? I know it's Penn State's team, but what *is* a Nittany lion? I know it's a lion that lived around Nittany mountain, but what's a Nittany? A place in Germany that they came from? A person just conjured up a funny sound?" Recently Nick was fascinated with the definition of "chimera." A chimera is a foolish, ethereal fantasy but a Chimera is a fire-breathing she-monster! Then there's the thing about the Christmas star having been seen in the east by the shepherds but in the west by the Wise Men who came from the east. Helen countered with her own question for him, "If you have three oranges and multiply them times nothing, how come the three oranges disappear?" That kind of illogical logic of hers always throws all of us math-men into speechless wonder.

On this occasion, since Helen was still jabbering in the kitchen, I had the honor of being the straight man. Thus my sleepy "huh?" was all Jube got to spur him on and it was, of course, enough. He volunteered that it's been proven that the first-born gets the best nipple nearest the sow's head and gets it every time for weeks afterward no matter how the piglets are turned around and mixed up. Scientists put numbers on their backs to prove it. "On the piglets' backs," Jube said. With the kids still staring at him, he feigned secrecy and whispered loudly, "They don't know what a teat is, do they? Anyway the runt gets the worst nipple. Good ol' survival of the fittest. What a system!"

I agreed with his analysis and showed him my sympathetic head-shake verifying disgust with "the system." Then the kids started arguing about the imitation feathers again, so I gathered them off to bed hoping I wouldn't be called upon to explain nipples, teats, runts and all the rest of our conversations. Luckily, they were tired children and happily nestled in bed with their nightly books, probably straining their ears for at least 20 minutes before nodding off. By the time I returned to my chair, Helen and Hannah had picked up their needlework, Jube was snoring, the black and white TV flickered an old movie.

I have always been slightly confused by Jube. He talked so earnestly about a myriad of subjects, yet he never described places he'd visited like Singapore. He just said, "You oughta go there someday. I never have time to sightsee, but I've sure seen some sights! Har-Har." Hannah was his perfect counterbalance. She laughed at his jokes even after she rolled her eyes and protested. When they had married, before we did, Helen was a bridesmaid. Hannah became Mrs. Jube E. Lant. Yes, she owned up to her sister, Jube was really his legal name. It wasn't short for anything. "Lant" was obscured in some murky heritage because he was an only child and his parents were dead. She loved him. So of course, Helen loved him too. And then I did. And then the kids did.

The Lants both worked at the Ex-Im Trade Company in Milwaukee and hoped to someday own the business which had six employees. Richer by far than we were, they invested in gems that adorned Hannah's ears and fingers, and we couldn't tell which were precious, semi-precious, man-made, or costume. We would guess: Fifty green stones in a necklace are not jade, at least not good jade. Jadeite? Nephrite? We didn't know much about stones. Hannah would reply to Helen's praise of, say, a bracelet, with "He was gone five weeks for this," and then she'd smile appreciatively at Jube. Helen would not ask anything else, and I thought I had better keep out of this sister thing. Even sisters like to keep some facets of their lives in a locked area, although they like to dangle the key in front of each other. Helen had a fine pearl necklace I had given her, but she wore it about once a year when we went out to dinner and made as long an evening of it as we could, dallying until we were sure the sitter had put our dear children to bed. However, Hannah never wore the same jewelry twice to our house. And what's more, she suddenly became interested in rock-hounding. Since a rock is lowest on the scale of price, I admit I was surprised. So now she put her knitting, or crocheting, or whatever tonight's project was, on the table and went to their bedroom and came back with an assortment of her latest acquisitions: geode, tiger-eye, lapis lazuli, jasper, fossils, and others I couldn't identify.

Helen was fascinated. I knew right then that next summer we'd be out hunting rocks at rock shops and Petoskey stones at certain secret shorelines of northern Lake Michigan, that beach stones would find their way into the collection, and that all of this would require support systems: tumbler for beach stones, sander and belts, polishing powders and washing machine motor for the Petoskeys. All of it would be bolted and arranged on "her" end of my workbench. Nothing's more invigorating than tramping in a quarry on a hot summer day, spitting on stones to see if their "eyes" revealed their identity. I have to admit, though, as avid campers we did enjoy being outside with a special mission. Eventually each of us found some truly exceptional specimens and felt quite proud. Helen kept them in their natural shape, bemoaning the bad stones cut into shapes of the state or animals and sometimes made into clocks. "I threw better stones than that out in the woods for the neighbor kids to find," she said. We never heard that any did. Probably TV and computers came along and replaced prowling in the woods with soporific activity.

One stone that Hannah brought from the bedroom was

amber. Worthless-looking hunk of epoxy, I thought. Rubbing it did indeed induce an electric magnetism of sorts but it always looked like glue to me, unfaceted, no sparkle. At least the flash of an opal suggested magnificence, but a piece of a bug caught in tree sap just never held my attention. Given all that, Jube seemed to share Hannah's enthusiasm for it, but he never gave her any. She never wore amber jewelry. Helen remembered a long, flapper-girl style amber necklace their mother had worn when they were children, and Jube excitedly asked what had happened to it. His voice caused everyone to look at him. Even our Llewellyn setter, Patch, stopped in mid chomp from chewing on his blue, rubber ball. It was, as they say, an auspicious moment but it passed quickly. Hannah recovered by saying that she only remembered the fox boa that frightened her with its mouth biting its tail around their mother's throat. Helen added, "With those beady eyes! Can you picture that fox with my red coat!" Hannah replied in her best uppity imitation, "I believe it's mink you wear, dahling." They laughed and laughed as we passed some smooth amber stones back and forth.

The fox started us on "what makes something valuable" such as salt's role in history; all that's left of that value is "He's not worth his salt." So we bantered things around, interrupting each other as friends tend to do, and passed another sociable evening. After we went to bed, Helen wanted my opinion on whether I thought amber would ever be valuable, and, if so, when. "Heck, it's used to make a gazillion pipe mouthpieces," I said authoritatively so as to squelch any ideas she might have of going out and investing in amber. You never can tell what two strong-willed sisters might concoct.

In the morning the Lants rushed back to their jobs, I went to work, and Helen fell back into her whirlwind world. There'd be three or four months before the Lants would resurface with a letter or a phone call, so, as usual, we were busy with our own interests and they were busy with theirs. We always assumed that we were busier than they were, what with two kids and a dog to consider, whereas they just up and considered what they wanted to do. At least that's what we thought. We really never knew what they did.

But as I said, we now had a dog to complicate and/or complete our domestic picture. I was used to doggie ways, having had a Blackie or a Sam or a Chester most of my growing-up years. Each one was an outdoor dog. Each one never saw a vet. Each one slept on the back stoop so I had to step over it when I came home late. Sometimes a dog would get into the house and make one swift circle in every room before getting thrown out again. Not that they were mistreated. We loved our dogs, and we petted them and fed them and played with them, and they were dogs. On the other hand, Helen never had a pet. Well, she had a black kitten for one summer but she had to give it back to the farm before winter. How could she "keep a cat in a house!" which is what her mother vehemently said. And she had two goldfish named Plunker and Dunker but doesn't remember their fate. But she never had a dog. Having had a dog, I wasn't even sure that this was the time to introduce that phenomenon to the household, so I joined her in delaying the decision while months of wishbone-snapping, first-star wishing, and other persecutions by the children would have us believe they *needed* a puppy:

H: Puppies are like babies. They cry a lot and get sick and do many BMs and grow into *dogs*.

Eliz: Did I when I was a baby?

H: Did you what?

Eliz: Did I cry a lot?

H: Yes, and you wouldn't eat and I was tired …

Jack: Did I too?

H: Yes, and sometimes you were sick and …

They had cornered her, left her with her faulty syllogism rattling. How could she compare a puppy with her darling babies! Moreover, could she cater to a puppy just when she had been given two hours of free time each day while the kids were in school? A puppy? A puppy? The living symbol of Home, Heart, and all the happiness and sadness they promote?

Desperate for some guidance that she couldn't get unprejudiced from me, she took her problem to a panel of experts on all matters of the heart and home: girls' bridge club. Stories about carpet-cleaning, barking, illness, biting, wandering, shots, mounting, chewing, ad nauseum, literally, filled her report to me. It reminded me of the same sort of advice she got from the same panel about pregnancy, which I had kidded her sounded like a story in the tabloids like "Unnatural Births In Your Backyard!" Come to think of it, she had almost the same reaction to both reports: she got curiouser and curiouser. So one April Sunday we got a puppy, a white with black spots puppy, a puppy with long legs and clumsy paws and a very frisky attitude.

That April Monday found Jack and Elizabeth in a state of blissful shock as they rushed off to school to spread their news. I went off to work. Helen spent the day trying to prevent accidents on the living room carpet. As she put it, she spent the day opening the door and going out and in with the puppy, or keeping her foot still while the puppy slept with his head on her shoe, or feeding the puppy the puppy the puppy.

But Patch, the one-black-eyed Llewellyn setter, blissfully unaware of all the anxiety surrounding him, just gained in length, stature, monkeyshines, and understanding. He learned to drop stolen socks, and his rat-tail tail developed a long, feathery fringe. Needless to say, we were fascinated by him.

Patch thrived on the kids' attention and soon was climbing in their beds to awaken them by putting his cold nose against their necks and pushing them over so that he could snuggle on the pillow, leaving, in exchange, sprigs of hay from his bed, which was

in a fine house I built within the protection of the garage and with a run outside its door. He was already more spoiled than any dog I ever had. Then all three would come out to the kitchen for a shared breakfast to start a shared day of summer. Only one game Patch invented and played alone: the Big Fly Hunt. We think he was sharpening his hunting instinct by finding a fly in the house, pointing at it, approaching it slowly and then chasing it until it landed on some chair. Then the entire routine would begin again. We let a fly or two remain in the house just for him—or us?—to be amused. The only problem he had was when the fly chose to land on the ceiling. Patch then walked on his hind legs, leaped in the air, and had such a general fit that we finally had to swat the fly. No one elected to swat the dog instead.

Helen resisted adding "Patch" to the Christmas cards, but the girls in her bridge club smiled condescendingly at her puppyisms and warned about being housebound with him when the January snows arrived. Patch fooled them, though. He joined me and the kids in our snowshoveling endeavors and went spelunking in our footprints. Once he went so wildly around and around the house that his feathery tail whipped in circles in the snow, fashioning perfectly round baseball-sized snowballs down his hind legs' feathered "pantaloons." Patch stood still while Elizabeth and Jack melted the snowballs with warm water. He seemed to sense that he needed help if he wanted to get outside and run again.

Running gave him his highest high, especially when he had the entire 20 acres of The Land we had outside town to explore and especially since that 20 acres had no fence around it. He could expand its borders, which he did every night after supper in decent weather and maybe three times a week in winter, rain, or wind. The routine never varied: I would finish the newspaper at which point Patch circled himself in uncontained anticipation. I'd open the hatchback of the Chevette and Patch would jump in quivering excitedly and then, as I'd adjust my seat belt, he'd give me a quick, cold lick on my right ear that made me jump every time. It seemed to be his important part of the procedure that made the car start. At the Land he'd hang around the garden and run along the edge of the drainage ditch until I got busy. When it was time to leave, I'd realize he was nowhere in sight and I'd have to busy myself for 15 more minutes that would be interspersed with loud calls and angry admonitions. Then he'd show up with his tongue hanging as if he'd had to turn on the afterburners to get back from his distant run without letting me guess just how many miles away he'd actually gone. His tail and the long hairs from belly and ears would be covered with prickers and dirt, which would make him very happy, and his tail would swish with glee on the drive home. There, after a hosing off, he'd lie on the living room carpet while Elizabeth snipped off prickers and Jack made a continuous distraction by patting him and talking calm reassurances. Later he'd spend many minutes biting the prickers and mud lumps from his padded paws. No one ever touched his paws. They were his running machines that he kept in perfect condition, free of mud and prickers in summer and free of ice chunks in winter

When Jack got a paper route, Patch of course thought it looked like fun, and he wanted to tag along. His talent of disappearing to faraway places, however, kept Jack from inviting him. Patch complained loudly to Helen, who would then chain him outside. There he'd continue to complain to our ever-patient neighbors that he had been left behind again. One winter Jack got the idea that perhaps Patch could have fun pulling a sled with the newspapers tied to it, so he hitched him up to the old Flexible Flyer. Away they flew, not exactly like the down of a thistle, more like a tumbleweed. Patch finally learned to go close enough to each house so that if Jack held a few papers at once, and if Patch waited now and then, the two of them were successful in the delivery of some 57 newspapers. However, it turned out to be more work and delay for Jack even if it was fun for Patch, so after a few weeks the partnership was broken. You'd have thought Patch's heart was too the way he carried on complaining.

Of course, as much as Patch entertained us for 12-1/2 years, there were quite a few times that he made us worry about him. He'd run away, and Elizabeth and Jack would call and hunt for him in the dark with flashlights and tears. Then he'd return wet, cold, and tired, but unabashed. The kids would be mad at him. He had insulted their kindness by running away. He had made them worry. But after a severe scolding delivered through their tears of relief, they petted him, consoled him, loved him. So it is with those we love: anxiety, relief, forgiveness, love. Always love. And, in Patch's case, Helen still had that respect for him that came out of the realization that he was an amazing compilation of feelings, instincts, and structure. He had toenails that moved in every direction; a muzzle that could tease a tiny ant or chew a shank bone with great cracking sounds; hair that always returned to its perfect curl after a rippling shake; short, white, eyelashes over large, brown, eyes; and a backbone that could be curled into a circle in complete comfort. All that, put together, accepted us totally different creatures as part of his world of happiness.

However, he had certain rules for us in order for him to be happy: We had to be *with* him, that is, within three feet of him and if he was running loose, we had to be within his radius so he could make it back to us at a full gallop within two minutes. That rule was bound to be stretched and broken by us—such as when we took him camping.

In deference to other campers who have a low level of appreciation for barking, we'd go camping in the rather unpopular month of October and set up on the far edge of the Hartwick Pines campground bordering the woods. We'd take hikes, with Patch keeping the 30-foot clothesline leash very taut. In the evening, he'd doze at my feet as we all sat around the campfire and talked about stars and satellites and stuff that was on the kids' minds from school events or whatever. But whenever one of us had to leave the site to walk the 100 yards to the facilities, Patch would stand up and bark so hard that his front legs would rise off the ground in emphasis.

He felt the same sense of extreme loss when we locked him in his pen and went skiing for the day. I know he felt very bad because once when we returned, a large, black, capital-lettered note was pinned on his gate: "THIS DOG BARKED ALL DAY." But what could we do? He'd tear the house and/or the camper apart in his anxiety if we left him alone inside. And we had to go skiing. It had been my idea to help pass the snowy winters and we had outfitted Elizabeth and Jack—then about 10 and 8—with boots, poles, and long skis. The tips touched the tips of fingers when the arm was held straight above the head. Helen and I still had equipment from 1956 including baggy stretch ski pants and special gloves for rope tows.

So that first winter of '72 or 3 we went to a small resort called Snowsnake that wasn't much more than an hour's drive and boasted four hills—one with a T-bar style lift. The kids took to skiing quite naturally. I taught them the basics that I knew: grab the rope tow with your right hand, and then twist your left arm behind your back and grab the rope and let the tow slip through your gloves or else an arm might get pulled from its socket. Never mind that people jammed in ahead of us, grabbing the rope with both hands in front and messing up the ski tracks on purpose so that our skis had to bounce over mounds and ruts.

Helen and I kept to the tried and true methods; although we had to brush up on our skills. Helen handled the tow rope easily, but she had to learn not to go straight down the hill. She had to learn to turn so she could traverse the higher hills, and the ones that I knew had moguls, the ones I'd hoped we could some day all ski together instead of separating into beginner and intermediate. So, I would ski down behind her and yell my directions for turning: "Up! Down! and Around!" She never did get what that meant, and when four school buses pulled up with junior high kids piling out in loud commotion, she retreated to the warming shack. During our home-packed, cold sandwich lunch, we watched the 200 kids through the steamed windows. They wore bright yellow, red, and green outfits and fell in every conceivable position onto the churned-up white snow. Helen said they looked like migrating butterflies that had landed on whipped cream and were frantically trying to free themselves. I was glad she found the scene enjoyable. She didn't join us for afternoon skiing.

By the following November, Helen's enthusiasm over skiing with rhythmic turns had waned. So for Christmas I gave her short, red skis, and we made a big deal of going way up north to Boyne Country where they had snow-making machines, a huge lodge—we parked our camper a few miles away—and chair lifts. When Helen looked up at those chairs swinging over the pine trees, she stopped smiling. "Isn't there another way to get to the top?" she asked.

Helen does not like heights. Ever since she had a panic attack at the top of the Arch in St. Louis when the kids and I were leaning over the slanted windows to find Busch Stadium "miles below," she has refused to climb anything higher than 15 feet and, since her white, sweaty face had scared us, too, we don't encourage her. The ski lift was a challenge. I told her that since it was a two-place lift, she'd have a chain on the side to grab.

As luck would have it, on this first day, a boy lurched onto the seat beside her and up they went. I watched her from the top of the hill, having been persuaded by the kids to make a few fast fun runs with them, and, to my alarm, I saw that one of her skis was dangling by its cord attached to the binding and around her ankle. The ski was off her boot! The guy in the lift control booth saw it too but was not alarmed—he just slowed the tow a bit instead of stopping it, and Helen jumped off successfully, falling clear of the onrushing seat behind her.

I helped her reclamp her boot while she gave me her tirade: "That little brat next to me was swinging the seat, leaning forward to yell to his friends, getting candy out of his back pocket, and guess what he is wearing! All 'Head' clothing! Even his striped cap! And guess where he's staying! With his parents and two brothers at the lodge! What young father can make enough money to put his family in the lodge for the weekend! And even *eat* there!"

I said, "They're probably in debt. What else could it be? No young couple could afford to buy the fancy RV parked next to our little canvas camper, either. It's probably rented, or borrowed, or something." Anyway, the familiar talk gave Helen a chance to calm down a little.

She stomped the ice chunks off her skis, adjusted her gloves, flexed her knees, and stood there. After all that excitement going *up* the hill, how would she ever go *down*? Just then a hot-dogger whipped off the lift in a wide stride and spun in a turn sending icy nuggets onto Helen's goggles. She whipped them off and berated the universe of modern discourtesy once more: "Look at that! No cap. No jacket. An earring! A neckchain! No manners." And then, with her goggles around her neck, she slowly started down the hill; I followed behind yelling, "It's easier to turn if you'd just ski faster!" I didn't hear what she yelled at me over her shoulder.

We spent many happy winters like that. So we had to deny Patch some of his wishes once in a while.

Now, from this vantage point, it's hard to realize that it's been more than 10 years since Patch came in for a drink of water after a Saturday run and collapsed. His memory, of course, surfaces often. When Jack went on a dog-sledding adventure in Minnesota, he said, "If I hadn't seen Patch's quivering with anticipation for his nightly run, I'd have thought our six sled dogs had some kind of disorder the way they were shivering, waiting to be harnessed." Elizabeth pats the little dachshund that visits her and feels instead the warm nose of Patch nuzzling her palm, asking for some of the ice cream that she most always had denied him. I could use a pal at The Land. It took me a long time to get over calling him to come when it was time to leave. And just yesterday, Helen said she was thinking about an art project to do in acrylic but she was "circling the bone," which is what Patch would do whenever we put a knuckle bone on a newspaper for him. He'd walk slowly around the edge of the paper, stretch out his neck to take a sniff, lick his chops, back off and slowly circle around again. After a couple more times of circling while keeping his eye on the bone, he'd finally lie down and take the bone between his front paws, crack off a piece of gristle and gulp it down in serious pleasure. "Circling the bone" became an apt description for our method of solving problems and making decisions. After Patch's collapse on that Saturday afternoon, we had to wait three days before MSU's lab work reported "poor recovery expectation, months of in-house care." I was at work, of course, when Helen had to tell the vet to give Patch the lethal dose. Elizabeth had been married a year but anticipated coming home at Christmas and putting the annual red bow on "her puppy;" Jack was studying for finals at college, looking forward to coming home and relaxing on the floor, watching TV, Patch's head on his chest. They were forever entwined: childhood, with Patch.

While the world was turning upside-down with the most shattering upheaval of law and order, the church's teachings, the family's calming and restrictive influences, and the school's steady goal of turning out people who were eager to "amount to something," we were calling our puppy and Jube was off to distant lands and Hannah waited and Nick survived an earthquake but had to rebuild his house. The four essentials we depended on for our children's futures suddenly ceased to exist. Even when The Bomb was dropped on Japan and Truman said it had to be done in order to convince the Japanese that we'd endure no more Bataans, most people continued to rely upon the structure of the home, church and school to reassure them that such a profound decision was indeed well-made. People kept the atmosphere of the era in perspective. The horrendous atrocity of war was over. A threat by Eisenhower ended the Korean conflict. Finally, we thought, finally there could be world-wide peace for our children. But that's when it happened. Just when we thought brotherhood had a chance to develop, our country exploded from *within*. Nothing had ever changed the USA more drastically than the sudden disappearance of respect—respect for parents, teachers, ministers, police, rules, regulations, and anything that had the whiff of authority.

The first hint that we could not escape from the new threats came when Elizabeth said marijuana could be bought at her intermediate school for $2.00 a plastic bag. The evening news was growing more and more violent. We were supposedly "deadened" to bloody brutalities since TV fought the war in our living rooms. Helen was very worried. At first I thought her reaction was exaggerated. We had a close family, a good family; we answered Yes to the question asked in the media: Do you know where your children are? But then more and more people at work said sons and daughters had quit school, left home—went to bring LUV to the world while leaving devastation at home.

Helen listened to advice from all the professionals who said "Sit down calmly with your children and explain the dangers … ." That didn't feel right to Helen: "First I'd scream and cry and rant and rave and *then* maybe I'd sit down calmly and talk. If I didn't rant and cry, the kids would think I'd been brainwashed or something. It's all too darn ego-careful. Like when that Ginott person advised sending a naughty child to his room and having him write down a list of things that annoyed him that caused his bad behavior. Lord! First off, the kids know they'd get a smack on the bottom. Maybe after that they could go write their lists!"

Helen's gut feelings were usually right. And she could always test them by presenting decisions to our "Potluck"—we met once each month for dinner at each other's homes. The women loved the chance to dress up and spread out their best china, and to discuss the raising of children. They each knew that little girls were different from little boys and that environment—giving girls guns and boys, dolls—would not change things a hoot. The child psychology experts were still studying this. We men just sort of hung around trying to keep things going as calmly and normally as we could. We turned down transfers that would have been job-enhancing but would have disrupted our families at a critical time in our lives. Meanwhile the world, as we and Mrs. Char and our entire generation knew it, was disintegrating around us.

The schools were caving in to the threats and chants of the students: We will tell you what we want to study; We want courses that lead to jobs; We don't want Latin and We and We, etc. What's worse, they were joined by college professors who *helped* them tear down traditions, traditions that are the backbone of an ethical society. Helen lamented, "Where is Confucius when we need him! He knew that good behavior comes from custom and example. So what will replace tradition?" TV brought us all the happenings, thereby transforming campus sit-ins and marches and "protest rallies" into big events.

Thus began the phenomenon of a minority getting its way over a majority. And could they ever swear! Girls and boys (I can't grant them false maturity as women and men) pronounced the sh… and fu… words as if they were newly discovered and needed to be used to start a new language. Those words sprinkled between "ya know" were supposed to show their new freedom to do and say as they pleased, I guess. We felt sad for them, sad that these students were not going to amount to anything. We pitied their loss of self respect. They laughed and spat at authority. They taunted police who had been caught off guard by "spoiled brats" and didn't know what to do until the confrontations grew and grew and became true violence.

Was all of this upheaval because of opposition to the war in Vietnam? Even after Johnson (America's "Dutch uncle" who would fix everything by throwing money at it) failed, and Nixon tried to ease the United States out of the war, the protests continued as if the reasons were forgotten. Congress withheld finances that would have helped to end the war, and when it finally ended, and the veterans returned, who did not give them honor? Their peers! Their own generation turned their backs. They scoffed at patriotism. The media analyzed these phenomena and decided America had lost its innocence. And we said, "Again?" America lost its innocence after WWI, after the Depression, after WWII, after mysterious bombings, after skyjackings, after anything that upset its equilibrium. And innocence will continue to be lost as each new generation meets a calamity.

Those years were our best of times (our children). And our worst of times (our country). We'd try to sort things out at dinnertime:

Helen: Evelyn's son John left home last week.

Jack: Where'd he go?

H: Nobody knows. Evelyn's called the police. She's frantic.

Eliz: Probably joined a commune somewhere.

H: Could be, I suppose.

I said, "There's the irony. They leave homes where they're provided for, and go where they say they'll be self-sufficient and end up begging on the streets."

H: I wonder what they think they contribute to mankind by doing the things they do.

Eliz: Mom, they don't want to contribute! You know, "Turn on, tune in, drop out" means "Take drugs, feel nothing, do nothing."

H: Horrible way to live. And the hippies I see look so unhappy.

"Most that we see are just copycats. They wear long, dirty

hair and ratty clothes so they look like they belong to the group that's getting all the attention."

Eliz: What are they mad about, anyway?

"I'm not sure they know anymore. It started about when you were born. I remember I had a business trip to San Francisco and there were all these sad, lonely, bombed young people sitting on doorsteps, smoking marijuana and taking LSD or cocaine or whatever. I thought that must be the most boring life there is. Even in the working world, if you get an assignment that you know is worthless, a sort of 'fill time' thing, it's harder to do it than to work."

Jack: The music isn't all that great, either.

H: Save me from Joan Baez. Something else I heard today: the high school cut out assemblies because students caused such a ruckus over who was invited to talk to them. I mean they cut out all assemblies, forever. Used to be we'd cut out the students. When was the last time you heard anyone say, "America is the best country in the world!" Teachers should emphasize that a Republic is a difficult but wondrous experiment, thanks to the wisdom of our forefathers, and needs everyone's support. Quit talking as if our mistakes are irreparable. It's vital that children absorb the overwhelming decency of our Constitution so they have the base necessary to build constructive lives.

"Well," I said, "we'll just have to do the best we can."

Our conversations didn't change the world, but at least they gave each of us a chance to vent our feelings.

Later, the 1960s group pulled children into its web of irreverent "rights", and any vibration of that web by Common Sense or the Reasonable Man caused them to scurry across and capture their victims with venom and litigation:

- Refuse to hire my son because he's got long hair and says obscenities? Show me the written law. To the courts you go.
- Throw him off the hockey team because he partied? To

From The Moon, Christmas Eve

Two men stood upon old fabled moon,
gazed back into the void, and witnessed Earthrise:
Moving like a child's lost balloon,

Earth dawned upon the alien ebon skies,
her bright surreal streams of blue and white
resplendent with the pulse of being alive.

They yearned to keep her close that Christmas night,
to grasp and hold the fragile cord of home,
of trees, snowflakes, children, colored lights,

but she turned away from them. Alone,
scuffing dust of untold centuries
like forgotten gods, they walked the lifeless dome.

The moon, unmoved by high technology,
blithely beamed their footprints back to me.

the courts you go.

- Expel him because he threatened a teacher? To the courts you go.
- Intercept my daughter's note offering drugs and search her locker without my written permission? To the courts you go.
- Write laws that define honor, decency, and respect. Spell everything out because everything that isn't written down is acceptable behavior.
- Interpret the first amendment to mean *every act* is a freedom of speech. Write it down! Write it down!

Leadership and guidance that used to be given by sensible parents, teachers, or ministers, was replaced with the legal vernacular of lawyers. The protesters became middle-aged and found that it was easier and more profitable to get their ideas enacted if they worked from "within the system." They discovered that they had to take responsibility now for the system they had so enthusiastically torn down 20 years earlier. The government of the 1990s—Woodstock In Shirts and Ties—ducked that responsibility. Can society become strong enough again to rescue its children from confusing, unsatisfying chaos? If the moon walk didn't alert earthlings of the fragileness of life and the urgency of having a friendly One World, what would? That Christmas Eve when we saw our blue and white earth floating in the black of infinity, we were awestruck. And we were saddened. I remember Helen's wishful thinking: "Why oh why can't we all just share everything, like Elizabeth and Shelly share all their Barbie stuff … ."

We, called the "jellyfish generation of the 1950s" because we hadn't marched against anything, again chose not to march; instead, juggling our lives between the happiness of our families and the chaos at their borders, we fought against depression. We decided the best thing we could do with this alien hobgoblin was to be steady. We would try our dardest to show that there still were more good people in the world than bad.

I still shudder remembering the confusion Helen and I had when Robert Kennedy was killed. We were awakened by our 6:30 alarm and were lolling in bed awhile listening to the morning music and weather forecast when an announcer said, "We interrupt your program to repeat: Robert Kennedy has died … ." We repeated, "Robert? Robert? But Jack Kennedy was just killed. But that was almost five years ago. This is Robert? Now Robert, too?" During the killing years, four prominent leaders had been gunned down and several more were wounded. We existed in a world we could hardly comprehend. And we had to raise our children and let them go out into that world!

It wasn't our first near-panic at child-raising. Helen had survived her first one when Elizabeth was born, overwhelmed with the responsibility of caring for a new person, new to this world. I had come home from work eagerly anticipating playing peek-a-boo and patty-cake with our happy infant, and there was Helen sitting on the floor surrounded with books and pamphlets.

I asked, "What are you doing? Research?"

Helen said she had to get some answers.

"About what?"

"Life. And Death. And Safety. And Health."

"What happened!"

"Nothing."

"Then what's the matter?"

"I don't want anything bad to happen to Elizabeth!"

"Why should it?"

"Well, just look at the world today! All god-awful stuff happening. And God is Love?"

I sensed this wasn't just another of Helen's philosophical exercises. I sat down next to her. "But, what bad thing are you worried about?"

"I don't know. I just feel I need to get answers quick before it's too late. I've been reading all about all the religions to see if God really keeps certain people safe even if He's a Spirit and we aren't."

"We could go to church again."

"Ministers always preach."

"Well, yes, they're supposed to."

"But they all preach as if they're reading the same newspaper headlines I read all week, giving us problems without solutions. They berate us for being egoistic creatures when really we just might be trying bravado. That plea, 'I believe. Help Thou my unbelief,' is the same as, 'I fear not. Help Thou my scared stiff.'"

"That's pretty strong, Helly. I used to like going to church. Coming home to Sunday chicken dinner."

"That was when you were a kid. Hank, you daydream in church!"

"It's peaceful."

"I read that every human need will always be met."

"That's good. What's wrong with that?"

"It certainly doesn't seem to be working. Every human need? In China? In all the Third World countries? Isn't it a human need not to be run over by the milk truck? I think I'm going to bypass all this guessing. Hank, are you listening?"

"I'm listening. It's just that Elizabeth is smiling at me."

"She's been cute all day. But, I mean, I think God doesn't watch us and send down stuff for us. I think God is just there like a Power and we have to plug in our little lights in order to connect, otherwise the Power just sits there ignoring us. But at least there's good music in Christianity, the most joyful and emotional music. Could almost make me think God listens and likes it."

Then Elizabeth, who had been watching our faces and hands and feet from her blanket on the floor next to Helen, decided she had lain there long enough. I scooped her up high above my head, and she opened her eyes wide and her mouth into a big Mason-jar smile. "Don't rile her up right before she eats," Helen said.

At the time, we didn't foresee that guns would be as available as pencils, and that people would decide guns were easier. We didn't foresee that illegal drugs would be the easiest way to make a lot of money. We didn't foresee that technology would spin ahead of spirituality; that a "gimme" society would decide life was fun and games; that sex would be declared a public sport. Just as Helen and I were struggling to avoid depression while we searched for a "good guy" and looked for the Man of Reason to come back and guide society's actions, along came two saviors: James Herriot, and The Land.

Helen giggled. She had returned from the library fuming about the "apostrophe-s" on the "New Release's" sign, but she had found a book about a vet from Scotland transported to North England and had thought with any luck it would have enough distance from the USA in 1972 to be refreshing. All of us liked to read books, especially in bed. We had ignored the child-rearing advice not to make a habit of bedtime reading "because then a child would not fall asleep without reading." So what?

We all read, and became anxious if we didn't have a horde of hoarded books to take on vacation, often reading by flashlight in sleeping bags, and always passing good books on to each other. Usually Helen and I followed authors. A need for a fat book would produce a Delderfield, Ayn Rand, Michener, Caldwell, or Irving Stone, with spy novels filling in while we rested from the meaty stuff. Stores selling used books were a must-stop on any trip and the AAUW book sales furnished our supply at home. Recycling was vital unless we wanted to build a warehouse addition. At the moment, I was reading another "cold war" thriller. Tension was building over sharing dried eggs in a bomb shelter.

So the giggle from Helen brought me out of this boring, even if true, chapter. I looked over at Helen on this dullest of evenings. Her eyes kept tracking rapidly across the page, her face had a relaxed and pleasant demeanor, her cigarette was smoking itself in the ash tray—all signs that she was on to something.

"What's so funny?"

Helen said, "It's this vet named James Herriot who gets his first job, and he's delivering a calf and these wry, Yorkshire farmers are kibitzing and—hee-hee—he's such a decent, patient, shy man and he's trying not to let them get his goat … ."

"Sounds different anyway."

She read *All Creatures Great and Small* and was sorry when she finished. I read it. Jack read it. Elizabeth read it. We recommended it to Potluck and bridge club friends. It delivered us from despair. It reminded us about good people who didn't drag each other to court. It was not fantasyland; it simply refused to be dragged down to the level of the worst side of mankind.

Helen wrote a thank-you note to the author, James Herriot, who lived in Thirsk amid the rolling Yorkshire hills. She said if she didn't thank him, she'd explode. And besides, she deeply felt that an author should be told when he makes people happy. Writing isn't easy, so appreciation is the second best accolade an author can receive; the best accolade is given by buying the book, of course. I agreed even though I wouldn't have the foggiest idea how to write a thank-you note to an author. Thousands of grateful readers knew how, and did. We were delighted to learn that we were not alone with our frustrations. Millions of people evidently yearned for stories of the values—unwritten, but totally understood—that are the cornerstones of a safe and healthy life, values that have absolutely no identification with the detailing of sadistic sex or the cut-by-cut descriptions of horrific murders that most editors seem to think is what sells.

Patch helped us to empathize with the love Herriot had for animals. For instance, one day Helen said, "Patch turned into a dog today. He ate baby rabbits he found at the side of the barn!" When Helen drove him home from The Land, he stood in the back of the Chevette with his head hanging over the front seat and above Helen's right shoulder, and she tried to rush home before he threw up or she threw up, and when neither did, she had to forgive him his doggie ways.

The atmosphere of Herriot's stories was always forgiveness and acceptance of each other's idiosyncrasies as part of being human—sort of like the relationship between Snoopy, Charlie Brown, and the Peanuts gang. And then, lo and behold, PBS ran "All Creatures Great and Small" as a weekly series from BBC. Then we had real faces from England to flesh out the individual images that were described so vividly by Herriot. When Robert Hardy, a.k.a. Siegfried, later played the role of Churchill on BBC, our reaction was that he was a very good Churchill, considering that he was really a vet! The actors caught Herriot's charm, pathos, and humor exactly right: Tristan doing his tipsy mad-conductor routine; Tricki-woo and the grumpy gardener; tricks the vets played on each other: imitating a farmer's urgent call for help with a displaced uterus at 3:00 a.m. Three more books brought the story to WW II and, thankfully, brought the veterinarians back to their practice, but the episode of James' leave-taking for war always made Helen cry and I admit I wasn't without some gulps. We looked forward to each episode like our parents had looked forward to listening to Jack Benny. Thank God for James Herriot.

The Land came to us at the same time Herriot did. We had been driving into the countryside for several years looking at swamps and farms—the kids wanted one farm that came with two horses thrown in—where I could get outdoors, away from my desk job, without the inconvenience of, say, skiing, which involved snow first of all and then lots of packing, driving, and expense. I think that was one reason for this longing for land, but maybe it was just a rationalization or an excuse such as "a good investment." Whatever, I wanted land. Most people we knew had bought a cottage up north, but maintenance is not my strong point and Helen was adamant that one house was enough. Actually we sort of had a second house in our tent-camper, which we hauled many, many miles during our summer vacations of two weeks. It didn't cry out for our attention when it was stored on a cement slab under Jack's bedroom window. We had come to a unanimous conclusion that land would be entertainment for everyone, including Patch, and wouldn't require our attention when we didn't feel like giving it.

It all came together one Saturday in November when Helen and I were trying to select a dining room table. For 15 years we had been hauling the kitchen table into the far end of the long living room whenever more than four people would be eating. Jack paged us at Miller's store and said the realtor had a parcel we might like. We rushed home, returned her call before she'd have a chance to put it up for grabs, and met her at the acreage. At the end of November our flat countryside, leafless with clumps of ice and dirty snow, looked very uninviting, but as we walked along the drainage ditch on the north boundary, the acres of woods on the east, the dirt road on the west, and the fenced fields to the south, I knew I had found my land. And being three miles from our house, it had location, location, location, as well as four acres of trees, trees, trees—the aesthetic requirement that Helen had insisted upon. So thanks to Jack's quick response and my vision of an apple orchard, we bought the 20 acres of farmland. We'd get the table some other time.

The Potluck group naturally became automatic partners in this endeavor, each family marking off side-by-side plots for gardens. Potluck now consisted of two cats, two dogs, eight adults, and ten children—friends who knew too much about each other to risk ever becoming enemies.

Even that many willing hands could not manage 15 acres, so

I rented that portion to a real farmer who planted and harvested his own crops and helped in emergencies. He pulled my rusty little Ford 2000 tractor out of the mud with his air-conditioned monster that barely had room to turn around in the field. In exchange, the farmer still gets to haul out fallen black ash for his woodburning stove. All in all, it's a good relationship. He's a good farmer—nary a weed in his/our fields, which makes him/us proud. I'm not bad either. The sea gulls have declared me legitimate by following in the wake of my plow and screeching to their friends "Come and get it! A farmer is plowing!"

The first spring brought a nice surprise: trilliums in the woods. There were hundreds, interspersed with yellow and blue violets. They were followed by false Solomon's seal, but by then the mosquitoes take over. The trilliums show up before the scrub brush gets dense and before the bugs wake up. What a sight! Helen phoned her friend, Phyl. They spent an hour walking around in the woods and considered themselves lucky people. That evening, I found "Beauty Is" on top of *Low-Load Mutual Funds* on my end table. I followed the punctuation the way I was supposed to and wrote "Nice" at the top.

Still, with all that unexpected beauty, we missed something vital to Michigan's winter landscapes: evergreens. November to June without greenery is just too long, so Helen planted 100 Norway spruce seedlings she obtained from the Soil Conservation District for a few dollars. We could be patient. All farmers have to be patient. We planted apple trees—some I grafted myself, I'm proud to say—with old-fashioned qualities: Bramley's Seedling—large, baking; Esopus Spitzenberg—Thomas Jefferson's full-flavored favorite; Lady—used for Della Robbia wreaths and eating whole; James Grieve—early eating; Cox's Orange Pippin ... and plum, pear, peach. There was spraying, pruning, mowing, harvesting, and canning. Helen canned applesauce, plums, peaches, but the four Moonglow pears that finally ripened we ate out of hand while looking over

Beauty Is

Nothing is prettier than a robin,
except, perhaps, a wren
singing vibrations like lace reeled from a bobbin
in unending delicateness. A hen
with quail chicks is lovely to see—
innocence tripping along behind pride.
Still, finches in full yellow are thrilling to me
like sundrops on grass. It can't be denied
columbine crowns of all colors are striking
and dandelions grow their own medals of gold,
yet pussy willows are much to my liking …

Beauty is in the beholder, I'm told,
but I know what beauty is—it's being unaware
of being, ignorant of splendor;
ingenuous volition unimpeded by care:
A butterfly pauses on any old fender.

the farmer's browning soybeans.

Of course the big farming equipment needed for my fun needed to be stored, needed a *barn.* It would not have taken much persuasion for me to quit my desk job in Personnel and spend the rest of my days digging the foundation shovelful by shovelful, but it was necessary to have money for lumber. I dug the foundation ditch shovelful by shovelful *after* work. And the exercise did keep me from getting frustrated. The two-car garage with an upper level became a true barn with a barn-shaped roof—the roof I contracted out to a builder whose men had falling-off insurance. At staining time, Potluck pitched in. Dick grumbled that his painting talents were more along artistic lines, such as painting scenes inside partridge eggs, but he slapped stain on the super-absorbent fake board and batten with the rest of the crew. A few cooling beers helped make the job easier, and it was finished in one weekend. Helen designed and painted a large hex sign with oak leaves and acorns within a circle of wavy lines, which she explained were symbols for good luck, good harvest, and good life for all of us. I nailed it on the front of the barn under the center window and under the colorful hex sign I nailed up four horseshoes that Helen had bought from a blacksmith in her home town in Wisconsin. With all of that goodwill and blessings and warding off of evil spirits, I declared us ready for anything.

That's what I thought. But Helen decided something was still missing. She said, "We need bird houses. How about a purple martin house? They eat mosquitoes."

I couldn't argue with that. Helen immediately went off to the local feed and grain store and came back with the biggest bird house ever made, barely liftable, redwood, with about 10 houses rolled into one! It needed a strong support pole. I managed to let two weekends pass before Helen's "Where are you going to put it?" got to me, so I lodged that palace in a cement foundation. Helen was happy, and two dozen sparrows and swallows chose to spend their hours fighting over it. Helen became unhappy.

"Guess what I figured out," she said.

"What?" I asked.

"The county started a spraying program," she replied. "There aren't any mosquitoes anymore except for in the woods and martins need swooping room so we could put the weathervane on the pole instead."

Darned if Helen wasn't right. I had read about the funds reserved for a spraying program but never connected it with food for birds. I put up the weathervane given to us by Elizabeth and Brad. It's a wrought iron English setter, on point. Elizabeth had said, "It shows where Patch has run away to." I liked it better than that overbearing house which I had hauled up the ladder and stuck in a corner of the upper floor of the barn. It was probably just a happy mansion for mice. But even then, Helen wasn't finished.

"Now we could use bluebird houses!" she exclaimed.

"There aren't any bluebirds around here," I retorted.

Helen agreed. "Of course there aren't. There aren't any houses! But they're seen at the Nature Center so I bet we could lure some here."

"I don't have time to build bird houses, Helly. It's either planting time or weeding time or harvest time."

"Well, over winter you could. This farming stuff has so much waiting! Watch and wait. Watch and wait. Next March we'll have bluebird houses, okay? That's when the males come to check out the real estate."

"Remind me around January," I said.

Summer officially began with Potluck planting tomatoes, peppers, and all the plants that required the danger of frost to be past, which made Memorial Day the perfect picnic/planting occasion at The Land. While thousands of people engorged the nearby highways to get up north to open their cottages for the summer, we drove three miles to the barn so we could move out the tractor, drag, plow, rototiller, and camper, as well as sweep out the dirt and dead flies from the cement floor and set up the collapsible metal table. We used to haul that table around for camping after too many episodes of eating off the hood of the car, but it became just another extra burden and finally was left in the barn. We placed the plentiful Potluck offerings upon it. The kids came running from the muddy ditch and we all set to. In a few weeks there would be sharing of strawberries, then gooseberries. "Is there a prickerless kind?" Then corn, tomatoes, celeriac. "Which part do you eat?" And parsnips. "If you want a muskmelon you have to accept some parsnips too." And there would be peas. "Who can find 11 in a pod?" And last of all, pumpkins, cabbage, pickles. You name it. Bounty: yup, that's the name.

As the kids grew up, their interests changed from dirt to blow-drying hair, and parents gave up their plots to have time to be coaches or spectators at whatever events required their presence. Steve continued by himself to plant his garden. He saved all the broken hockey sticks from his two boys' games and garnered enough of the broken pieces to mark all the rows in his garden, at the start of each row and at each end, for at least 15 years.

Eventually, weeds took over all the gardens but Steve's and mine. Helen and I recognized it was "that time again," time to change direction, time for the five-year shifting of gears again. With each five years, we grew in understanding of each other, which built a sort of platform on which we could stand together, just above the swampy, scary world.

In August, 1980 I think it was, Helen got a note from Hannah explaining that they would be leaving early for Florida this year. Jube had decided to do more traveling now that they were semiretired, and Hannah would hole up in their condo at Naples for the winter. Did we want to visit them there or in Milwaukee or what? We had to acknowledge that the road ran both ways—since the Badger and Spartan no longer docked at Milwaukee—and it probably was time for us to visit them. It was a familiar and boring trip whether going east or west on the expressway.

Helen suggested we take the northern route across the Bridge and have some interesting scenery but I objected to adding five hours to a nine-hour trip.

She pulled out the emotional angle. "But the Bridge was built in 1957 when the Lions got the NFL championship, Sputnik was launched, and we were married. Of all the bridges we've crossed, I really trust Big Mac the most."

I said, "Because, quote, the Mafia hadn't watered down the cement, unquote."

"Well, I like the bridge. It's beautiful. But I suppose we could save it for a color tour … ."

We drove around lower Lake Michigan to Milwaukee. We always liked being with Hannah and Jube; we just didn't like getting there. Jube would treat us to a dinner at one of the marvelous German restaurants—from Mader's in the city to the Fish Shanty in Port Washington—and over the years we'd been to them all. And then there was golfing on Jube's hilly Country Club course that had grabby greens instead of the pool-table effect we were used to.

The evening of our arrival we enjoyed dinner at Barth's. The next day we enjoyed 18 holes of difficult golf with our excuse being that we have no practice with downhill or uphill lies. And then we enjoyed Hoffmann brats grilled outside and eaten on true hard rolls, not the two-day-old rolls that pass for hard rolls at home. Wonderful! Hannah then invited us down to her inner-sanctum in the basement where the walls are lined with boxes and shelves holding beginnings, middles, and endings of all her many projects. She hauled out a wooden cigar box full of her latest treasures which turned out to be amber.

Hannah held up a bronze-colored stone. "Did you know that the best amber comes from the Baltic Sea area from a layer called "blue earth" made 50 million years ago? And that Stradivarius violins were covered with amber varnish?"

Helen gasped, "They crush them to make varnish!"

"Not the good ones. Just the dark ones with impurities. They heat them and distill out acid and stuff and use the pitch and linseed oil to make varnish."

"Look at all the colors. I thought amber was amber," Helen said.

"I've got opaque golden yellow all the way to almost transparent brown," Hannah said, while she lined up a few for our inspection. Jube held up a stone almost as large as an egg. "What do you think of this?" he asked, knowing it was the most impressive stone in the collection.

"It's gorgeous!" Helen exclaimed. But then Jube said, with a smile, "It's copalite. Not good."

"But it's good enough for earrings. I made some for you, Helly," Hannah said. She gave Helen teardrop clip-ons which Helen put on and I had to admit they looked nice. "I got hand cramps sanding them," Hannah added, "but at least they smell nice while I'm working on them. Like pine."

Helen and I both asked, "How come?" Hannah's explanation was fascinating. She said amber is tree sap, just as I had declared, and that it's usually pine. She sands it and it smells like pine. Then she polishes it with cigarette ashes. She uses a chamois cloth and the result is a golden glow.

Jube and Hannah had once again entertained us royally. We left the next morning since fish and visitors stink after three days.

On the long ride back home, I said that it was amazing how they had become encyclopedic with amber information and now even had a good collection. Of course Helen, liking any information, found it all to her liking.

"I really liked that amber," Helen said.

"I know you did."

"You didn't?"

"You know I didn't."

"I know. But at least it looks like now they have a common interest," Helen suggested, "and maybe they'll travel together for a change. Except, Hannah doesn't like traveling that much, and Jube can't sit still more than a month. Jube thinks your hobby of The Land is more work than working is. He'll probably never retire."

"Reminds me, our two rows of berries ought to be in blossom by now. Probably there'll be enough for you to can a quart or two," I said. Helen said two quarts wasn't worth the effort. So our thoughts left Hannah and Jube and their lives and returned to ours with a feeling of refreshment and invigoration. That's what visits are supposed to do: refresh and invigorate. And what's more, the 1980s were starting out pretty good. The hippie generation was getting to be 40 years of age. That, I thought, ought to sober them up.

'Course I forgot that they all had children, children who slept in their parents' beds until the age of ten, children who … I made myself stop the line of thought. Helen was dozing with her head against the window, and I drove past Lansing seeing not the road but the area at The Land that needed more drainage tile … probably 43 feet should do it … hard clay down there … use the pickax … .

September.

"We got carried away with apple trees, Helly."

"Walking around all day every ten days with a tank on your back getting to be too much?"

"Not only that. Well, mainly that," I admitted. "But we don't even like the Kandil Sinaps."

"But it's an old apple from Turkey, and oblong, and unusual, and pretty."

"But, you don't like to eat it, Helly."

"I like it to look at."

"Is this a working farm or an English garden!" I said.

"It's a farm working at being paradise. But you're right. While you're at it, I don't like that Lubsk Queen either," Helen admitted.

"The catalogs do embellish a bit."

"It's like wine-tasting. Metallic is supposedly a desirable feature of a wine's body or aroma or bouquet or whatever they call it. Maybe it's our weather. Maybe Cox's Orange Pippins are truly wonderful in England."

"Well, I'm going to pull some out. Ashmead's Kernel didn't do so well either. And that Moonglow pear that's supposedly heavy-bearing hasn't beared at all."

"But what will I sell on the street corner after you retire?" Helen teased.

I said we'd figure that out when the time comes. "Maybe you could sell raspberries. Specialty crops have less competition."

"You mean there will be other women on the street corners when you retire?"

"If there are, I promise not to notice … ."

From 76 apple, pear, plum, and peach trees I eventually pulled out all but 20 or so. Once in a while we still come across a variety we absolutely cannot resist trying, so we plant a Stearns, say, and like it. The orchard holds pretty steady at around 20 because others die before we get to try them. Helen's Lady apple bears alternate years, so every other year we get bushels of little apples that she eats six at a sitting and also cans like crab apples. She got the canning recipe through exchange with a reader of

Pomona, which is one of our connections with reality. Readers write not only of their successes but also of their failures, which they often ascribe to their own lack of knowledge or their enjoyment of risk-taking. It's refreshing, especially when compared to seeing startlingly beautiful photos in our catalogs that show brilliant 20 year-old wisteria vines but then receiving 14-inch, bare root specimen which tells us without words that we'll be lucky to live long enough to see how lovely this vine should be. Even the titles in *Pomona* are gripping: "Trellises: Pitfalls and Possibilities;" "700 Bushels of Applesauce;" "Canker-causing Fungi of Applewood." So when Helen wrote and asked what to do with four bushels of Lady apples, a woman wrote to her and enclosed the crab apple recipe while also asking for a scion from the Lady tree for which she sent the usual $1.00.

Helen's favorite woman's magazine pictured Christmas decorations using Lady apples. "Do shoppers actually find Lady apples in supermarkets somewhere?" she scoffed. We tried putting a few on grapevine wreaths, having our own source of both the apples and the vines, but they didn't last long enough to be worth the effort. Nevertheless, I'm sure I'll hear the same scoff when the next November issue arrives.

I spray, cut, plow, mow, dig, hoe, and stand out there and watch the geese >>>>>>> over my head. Last October, long sheets of them rose and fell from horizon to horizon. It's impressive, yet I think following a leader must be easier than what snow buntings do: a fat cloud of birds swoops here, rises, swoops there, lands here, rises and lands there—all synchronized. How do they do that without a leader?

Helen plants a few of her favorite things that are inexorably becoming unavailable: bittersweet, pussywillows, velvet leaf, partridge berries, sunflowers, and who knows what next. After each new planting, she gets another dose of awe: "Imagine! The seeds they found buried for 2,500 years, sprouted! What's in a tiny seed that it can rise again. Hank, doesn't that hint of a kind of resurrection? Isn't it scary?"

I replied, "I don't know if scary is the right word ... maybe reassuring?"

Helen ruminated on that and I'm glad for the silence. I don't know how she can be so basically cheerful with all those scary thoughts she has.

We've got The Land pretty well under control now, but there are, of course, moderating elements like having to haul water from home. There's no electricity either, but I hooked up the motion sensor device that Brad gave me. It stores energy in the screen on the barn roof and then when I enter the dark barn, a light goes on. It's a relief not to scrape my shins on the plow blade anymore. I guess we're sort of the "Good Neighbors" type but not as full-blown afflicted as the BBC couple; we're just self-reliant enough to keep it fun. So the neighbors and good friends think we're a bit "touched." They thought that about me when I preferred to go camping instead of vacationing at a luxury hotel. "Where are you going to make it rain this time, Hank?" they'd smile when I'd leave for vacation. Unluckily, it is too often true that I can even make it rain on a ski slope in January as easily as on a tent in July. But at least vacations were always unpredictable, and that was a lot more fun than predictable.

There are times when Helen would like to be a bit less Spartan and have a little TV along in our little 19' trailer, which is our upgrade move from our tent camper. For instance, the times when she catches a radio disc jockey saying "... severe storms with damaging winds and possible hail in the listening area, so keep tuned to your favorite station, that's beautiful WQQQ, and we'll keep you posted ... Now back to easy swing on beautiful WQQQ." Then she slams down her needles and hollers, "And where the heck *is* 'beautiful WQQQ'! I can get Florida in South Dakota, for crying out loud. How am I supposed to know where the weather *is*! Isn't there an identification rule for radios! The young girl in the office doesn't even know the frequency of the nearest radio station. She doesn't even know what a frequency is! Everyone has a TV!"

That situation bothers her. The other thing about storms that bothers her is that I usually fall asleep. Somehow I can't get an adrenaline rush from a storm. I recite all the statistics about percentages of tornadoes hitting right where we are etc., but it makes no difference to her. A memorable storm hit our camper last summer. I was in bed, reading. Suddenly Helen stopped knitting and yelled at me, "Get your pants on!"

"Why? Are we going somewhere?"

"I don't know! Just get 'em on! The wind's really strong. We're really rocking!" So I got 'em on and looked out the window.

Helen's voice rose with the wind, "Why are you looking out the window? It's dark! If we survive, you'll say 'See? Nothing happened.'"

"Helly, what am I supposed to do? Even if we tipped over, so what?"

"So what? So what? So we'd be killed!"

"We'd just tip over."

"All the canned goods would fall on our heads. Remember that tree at Traverse City? It fell and smashed a trailer."

"Nobody got hurt."

"Luck. Just luck."

"Well, this one's just about over. The wind's dying down."

Helen was still berating the radio. "Detroit announces where it is. And remember Mitchell, SD? I should write them a thank you. I could trace that storm all the way on the map. It was a great job they did, even interviewing sheriffs at the scene."

She might have said some more, but I had opened my book

and could barely feel my cross-stitched "This Is Where I Fell Asleep" bookmark slide off my chest. When Helen crawled in next to me on the narrow couch that the salesman said "opens into a double bed" but is actually a wider narrow couch, I put my arm across her, patted her fanny in acknowledgment that I knew she was with me safe and sound, rolled over to turn off the trouble light I read by, and then I recognized that she was not yet down from her brush with death-by-tipping-over, for, as if an hour hadn't passed, she said "… and that's another thing you don't do by the book!"

"What book?" I asked, truly innocently.

"Not any specific book. Just all the books I've ever read." Now that was irrational even to someone half asleep. She was upset about something and I'd better find out what or else *she* would be asleep and *I* would be awake. I said, "The storm was over when I fell asleep. Nothing happened."

"In every book I've ever read the guy comforts the girl—he doesn't quote statistics—brains have nothing to do with emotions and reasoning never does away with fears."

"What do you want me to do?"

Helen replied with slow emphasis. "No guy ever, in all the books I've read, ever gets up and goes to the kitchen and gets a hunk of cheese and brings it to bed and turns on the light and eats it and reads … ."

"Eats the l … ."

"Eats the cheese! The cheese!"

"Oh, guys don't eat cheese during storms?"

"I'm not talking about storms," Helen said.

"What *are* you talking about?"

Helen lowered her voice. "After making love, the guy is supposed to cuddle and whisper adoration in the dark."

Oh, oh. I opened my eyes. There was some connection here between storms and … cheese; no, storms and guys; no, lights and … all the books about guys … I thought I had better try levity: "So you're saying I'm not like any other guy you ever heard about?"

"Oh turn out the light."

I did as I was told, rolled back and placed my arm gingerly across her side. She took my hand and held it still. Whatever that conversation was about, I guessed I had a reprieve if I didn't try to move my hand. Probably, I reasoned illogically, I just missed some important cue word. She's so darn aware of words. I often forget what I've read, even read some books twice that seem familiar but are still vague, but I don't learn a whole lot of profundities from books. Except that one on bass fishing.

The storm had cleaned the morning air. Birds happily found worms nearer to the surface. Rabbits had "dressing" on their dandelions in the form of water droplets, and ate them from the stem end up to the blossom, which boinged up and down the closer they got to it. The truck didn't need me to wash it; the camp office got newspapers by 7 a.m. So there we were, eating raised sugar donuts, drinking drip coffee and reading the paper. It was a clean morning of contentment with not a hint of any surprise test-question on last night's big and little storms.

Suddenly Helen snapped her paper.

"Dining at it's finest! I, t, apostrophe-s! Do editors have to accept ads with errors? Doesn't anybody proofread anymore?"

Aha. The apostrophe syndrome struck again. It drives her crazy. Over the years she's resisted dashing off irate letters. "Too old-maid-English-teacherish," she explains. Nevertheless, a couple of times the error was too flagrant to ignore. For instance, a pattern company in its pattern book distributed to sewing/material stores across the nation printed patterns designated, "Sweaters, His and Her's." Helen came home from the store and asked me how many people did I think that layout was approved by. "Their business is communication!" she lamented. So she sent off a letter that explained possessive pronouns. She got a nice letter back that thanked her and enclosed coupons for two free patterns, but more important to her was that the next season's issue had the mistake corrected. The other incident was the packaging of Chedo's. She wrote explaining possessive nouns, explaining it wasn't Chedo's, it was Keebler's Chedos, a simple plural. She got a letter saying that their grammarian approved Chedo's. She wrote back that they should take a look at Fritos. Within six months the boxes on the grocery shelves displayed Chedos. "Packaging is their business of communication!" she moaned.

The produce departments in grocery stores give her acute apostrophe shock. Just reading "banana's, 4 lbs. / $1.00" right next to "lemons, .29 ea." makes her shudder and restrain herself from grabbing the manager by his apron and asking "What do bananas own that lemons don't?"

Some situations have been downright funny. We toured The House of Seven Gables. In the yard the trees were labeled. One was labeled "hawthorne." We laughed. Helen went into the museum office to tell the ladies at the desk that she appreciated their joke. But the ladies had no idea what she was talking about. Since then she's noticed nursery catalogs advertising hawthorne trees. "Hawthorne added the 'w' to his name but always had the 'e.' The tree has no 'e'!" she complained again to me. But it does in many, many places, including Hawthorne's hawthorne tree in the yard of The House of Seven Gables.

We once had the notion that we could become word-watchers during our camping trips and compile a book on the museums, plaques, signs etc. that have blatant errors carved in stone, but there were so many that we decided it would be too depressing and the book would be too thick. If only the officials in these places would take criticism constructively and change the errors as the pattern company did, Helen would be happy. But the officials usually just look at her as if to say, "Who cares?" So we find

- resorts offering accomodations
- big billboards blaring Camping at it's best
- headlines screaming, He gets his just desserts
- Disney selling wooden identification signs: The Wilson's
- stores hanging signs that direct the customer to Stationary
- TV people saying Between he and I …

Helen says the newspaper people have computers and deadlines to blame but that it's odd that their errors are identical to the ones used everywhere else. One could think a conspiracy of people who demanded job relevancy for their education are now having jobs as proofreaders. I don't take it as personally as Helen does, but I agree that trying to read anything these days is like trying to walk down unequal steps on a stairway.

When Helen's newspaper snapped, I knew it would be followed by some verbal snappiage. I know there is no such thing as an "ex" English teacher even though that's what she was called after our marriage. So while she was snapping away, I went mentally off and mused over the interesting items she had pointed out to me, or questioned me about, over the years:

She likes the FALLEN ROCKS signs on highways much better than the FALLING ROCKS.

She thinks pronouncing raspberries as "razzberries" is wrong and would like the authorities who write dictionaries to notice that "rasp" refers to the sharp, raspy points on the canes, whereas "razz" is a ruffling tongue of disrespect which raspberries do not deserve.

She wonders if cavemen whistled happy tunes.

She's waiting for archaeologists to find the shards that reveal what dinosaurs worshipped.

She laughs whenever the most repeated line on her soap opera comes up again in response to "I love you," which is "Do you really mean it?" or "Do you mean it? Really?"

Thinks the funniest line in a sitcom was on the Mary Tyler

Moore show when the MC at a fundraising dinner introduced an amateur tap dancer by saying, "And now we ask the musical question, 'Steam Heat.' I didn't get it then and I still don't get it.

The Name Of The Rose raised the question whether all animals that have four stomachs have no front teeth. She wrote to Faith, a high school friend who is a dairy farmer and who had to pry open a cow's mouth to get the answer which was "No, they have no top front teeth," not that anybody cared. It was just another curiosity that had to be pursued to the end.

According to Helen, the most often misspelled author's name is Edgar Allan Poe. Even on a poster in the library and in a 1994 WWII war-in-Italy-type book that was impeccable except for that, and worse, on a book jacket proclaiming that the author had won the "Edgar Allen Poe Award."

She reads strange sentences to me: "I pulled open the outward swinging door," and wonders if the author would also write, "I pushed in the inward swinging door," or if a mediocre author would write, "I opened the door"?

She says that the best sign ever painted is, FORM TWO LINES. I agree with that, at least.

She insists that a man still feels superior when passing another car and that the phenomenon stems from the days of the carriages when a man raced against his neighbor to show off his fine, matched team of horses, and his driving ability, and his fearlessness. She calls it the "Ben Hur Syndrome."

Whew! If my brain were full of all those things I wouldn't be able to concentrate on our taxes, investments, or bills, much less my golf game. But Helen does have a point. Stores should not hang up big signs that say "Mother's Day Idea's." I can hear Mrs. Char saying, "Sloppy thoughts become sloppy acts." World leaders do not say, "Ya know, uh, like I mean tariffs. Just between you and I, like, you know where I'm at?" Not yet, anyway.

Helen pitched the newspaper aside, and we decided to work out her frustrations on the golf course where we could kill off angst with some vicious strokes.

I had an inkling one autumn at the Land—after we harvested all the crops and the ground was eager to rest in peace under a cover of snow—that there was going to be another shift in direction coming up. It seemed like every five years something happens along the merry road we've been traveling. Sometimes it's a pothole-type happening like a job change or an illness; sometimes it's a big detour, a death. Helen's niece suddenly dying at age 30 leaving her husband and two little boys was too profound to absorb. A wild winter snowstorm preventing our going 500 miles to tell our deep sorrow, changed the tragedy into a mist-covered illusion of the mind.

The deaths of our parents occurred one by one and years apart. Helen's Mom spent winters with us for 25 years after her husband died. She who had a great fear of dogs learned that Patch would keep a polite distance from her, so he received a careful pat on the head after the first five years of distrust. Although we were frustrated that she couldn't resist training our children, she also knit fancy stocking caps and mittens for them. She loved to bake sweet Schneckens and we loved eating them. Once, she gleefully made "stolen Stollen" with apples she and Helen picked from someone's neglected tree.

But, her loneliness led to reliance on Helen's companionship, a companionship that often overwhelmed Helen's attempt to be a daughter while being a wife, mother, and sister. The closeness lasted so many years into adulthood that there was no normal and gradual weaning away of daughter from mother. That made the final separation harder rather than easier, even though this time, unlike with Helen's decision for Patch's death, I was with her when she told the surgeon that it was time to give up. We still see him walking down that long hospital corridor after he wrote "pain only," folded his paper of instructions in half, and gave us no word of comfort.

So when our last parent died, we were struck by the realization that we both were without a mother or father. We were alone together. There are places in hearts reserved "parents," no matter where we are or what we have become. When parents die, those places are empty, never to be filled with anything else. It doesn't matter how or when death comes; it doesn't matter that we are luckier than most people; it comes. And a new, strange loneliness occurs because there is no Mom or Dad to phone for reassurance of an ineffable love. Even if the children are estranged from parents, or if old age turns the tables and the children becomes the parents, the awareness of the existence of parents remains. When only memory remains, it takes a long time for it to have any substance. Death is the inscrutable truth that is, irony of ironies, called a fact of *life.*

That autumn was pleasantly warm. The maples in the woods put on a strikingly beautiful show. There was no obvious reason for me to feel uneasy. I decided I had given in to the old Puritan heritage that doled out revenge just when a person was feeling smug over his fortunate life. In spite of misgivings, we went on with the usual plans for the holiday. Helen phoned Hannah.

"Are you coming for Thanksgiving? It's your turn, you know."

"Jube wants to leave early again this year," Hannah said. "How about late October?"

"Sure! Whenever it suits you!"

So they came. And Jube crawled out from behind the wheel, exaggerated a cramp in his back, and asked, "Why do you live so damn far away!" No kids were around to giggle, both being in college, so Helen and I giggled. Then Hannah brought in the bag of gifts that she had painstakingly created: crocheted snowflakes hanging from a crocheted center—replacement for the rock-slab

With Sympathy

"Words cannot express . . ."
Yet now, as always at the end,
they must.
Outpourings of sympathy
wash over my wrinkled soul
until at last, words come
to say what tears could not.

chimes in the living room—as well as a tiger-eye tie pin to give to Jack and a beautiful lamb for Elizabeth's bed menagerie.

And then Jube asked me to help carry in a box. It was heavy, made of wood, and about five feet long. This was not a case of good beer; it was not a case of summer sausage or bratwurst. We stood it up in the living room. "We'll install this tomorrow," he said, as if the box was not at all an aberration from our usual routine.

After dinner we settled into our usual chairs, with my perfectly-built fire flaming calmly in the fireplace as if it were one of those new gas-fired logs. I expected a light-hearted conversation sprinkled with some of Jube's slightly "off" jokes, but somehow it turned depressing. Hannah accidentally started it by reporting that her friend's husband had died; Jube added that their neighbor had cancer. I kept losing the thread of the recital of agonies. I was looking at the box. It was so close to the fire. Would it warp? But Jube carried on with his proclamation that the world was a lousy place, that death and agony were everywhere and had been since the dinosaurs. I admit I don't like to talk about those things. Helen and her Mom regularly used to regularly rip apart the Whys of existence. So did Helen and Jack. I don't like unanswerable questions, and I don't think it's because I have a scientific mind, as Helen insists. I stood up to shake off depression and give a distracting toast "to the box," but Helen stood up simultaneously. My beginning toast "to the box" was landed on by her proclamation, "Man landed on the wrong planet!" I sat down again, took a sip of manhattan, and girded myself for her soliloquy.

H: Dinosaurs tanked around for thousands, millions of years, and I think that was plenty long enough. But the thing that worries people is how long is long enough for us? Us humans. If you position yourself above the earth like a low astronaut able to see everything, what would you see people doing? You'd see all the roads jammed with cars moving with great speed in all directions exactly like an anthill—no obvious rhyme nor reason. Every city from St. Paul to Brownsville, from Maine to Baja [not cities, I said to myself] have roads streaming with cars, the bridges crumbling, the sewers crumbling, [she's veering off] and all the hospital parking lots full. You'd see uncountable murders, robberies, fights, fires, floods, quakes. The globe would look like one gigantic murderous, fornicating, dying, struggling agony. Do you know anyone who is healthy? Who has no allergies, arthritis, migraines, cataracts, hair loss, cancers, asthma, psychological derangements, muscle ailments, bone ailments, skin ailments, and pain, pain, pain. [She got my attention. I got a new drink.] You know what else you'd see? Monkey Island. Monkey Island in the human condition. Monkeys groom each other, and we laugh. But if you look down upon this earth you'd see the people in the barber shop, the dentist's chair, the hairdresser's shop plus its manicure, pedicure, hair removal and ear-piercing departments. Look at the podiatrist, ophthalmologist, allergist, doctors of every bone and orifice. Like monkeys with serious demeanor we groom each other, and after we've groomed we kill each other. Has there ever been one day of total peace on earth since the Beginning? All life exists on death, and Nature is our example. Annie Dillard studies Tinker Creek—one long chain of animals eating each other. And it's not always true that they only eat the sick or the old for the benefit of the survivors. Anteaters eat any ant they find, don't they? Birds eat any worm? [God, Helly, what are we supposed to say!] Even the Farmer In The Dell has its chain, its natural pecking order, and the cheese has its fermentation process. The cute Marsh Wren destroys the eggs of the blackbird that is her neighbor in the reeds; a certain snail eats its siblings before they're hatched; 80% of chickadees die during a hard winter. If the loving God counts every sparrow, His record book must weigh tons. Jonathan Edwards said, "we hang by a slender thread," and he was right. It breaks every second for someone somewhere, no matter if he prayed or not, was good or evil, or was two months old and too innocent to know he was alive. If the gods would listen to Earth, they would hear moans, groans, wailings and the high laughter of the mercifully insane. We landed on the wrong planet. The earth is hostile to us. The dinosaurs fit it better.

She sat down and looked at us.

There was dead silence. Helen had, bless her, gone past what we were willing to accept as question/answer for the evening. She suddenly realized it too, and bless her again, she stood up and asked, "Herring, anyone?" We jumped up together as if catapulted by the same spring, went to the kitchen and stood around talking refreshing nonsense about the chance of rain tomorrow while Helen dished up creamed herring with crackers and I refilled our drinks.

The phone's ring was like lightning at the window. Helen recovered first and managed to get to it before the answering machine answered. She said, brightly, "Hello? Oh, Nick! Yes, we're fine. They're here. Hannah's fine. What's happening with you? … You just have to bite the bullet instead of sitting around freezing all winter. We've only replaced the fan four times so far on our new furnace … ha."

We three went into the living room, leaving Helen jabbering happily for 30 minutes. When she hung up she was smiling and relaxed, her deadening speech to us having left no furrowed brow on *her*.

She reported, "The question for today is, 'How do mammals, specifically porpoises, breathe when sleeping at the bottom?' And the answer is they have to come up for air every five minutes and it makes Nick tired. I told him they don't wake up each time and have coffee and say, Damn, now I'm awake again!" We laughed a pure laugh this time.

I thought, What an alien mind she has! But out loud I said,

Wedding Of Our Daughter

Someone wants her.
Though we would not sell,
she shall be bought and taken
from our wild possession.

We are but traders
dealing in Love.
Like simple merchants
we sign farewells
in quick transaction:
now ours; now yours.
We gamble with life,
sell a portion of our souls
without bargain—
just a handshake,
an embrace.

"Here's to monkeys and porpoises!" and we all laughed again as if showing our teeth would deaden the truth of the night's insights. "I hope I didn't depress you," Helen added, "because my own philosophy is Put The Garbage On The Curb." I guess that was supposed to clear up everything, but nobody asked what she meant for fear of getting an explanation. So we went off to bed. I don't know if Jube and Hannah had nightmares in their bed in Elizabeth's old room, the room they'd known as hers ever since her babyhood. When they turned out her lamp with the pink shade and the wooden little girl and lamb on it, did it give them a pang to realize Elizabeth had grown up and gone away?

Helen and I snuggled against each other in our old, familiar double bed, and then Helen sleepily said, "I wonder what's in the box?"

Finally I could unleash all the musings I'd been having! I said, "Whatever it is, it didn't ooze onto the carpet. It's really heavy. Maybe a wrought iron stand of some kind. But why wait if it is, and Jube acted possessive of it, as if it had more to do with him than with Hannah. How come you didn't pump your sister for a clue? Helly? Helly?" Rats. For a minute there I thought she'd want to get up and examine the box in a scientific manner, gauging its weight, diameter.

I was up first, 7:00 being set on my farmer's internal clock, which rang on weekends the same as the rest of the week. Today, Saturday, I was up at 7:00 circling the box a la Patch's method. No clue. So I started the bacon and soon had three customers for a hearty breakfast and lots of black coffee.

It was during the second refill that Jube prompted, "So. You ready to haul the box to The Land? You comin' girls?"

The box was so heavily on my mind that I fleetingly thought of faking "Box?" but I didn't want to get a big eyeroll from Helen, whose intuition and experience told her that last night's

diatribe had not moved me from wondering what the heck was in it. Was it just a big Jube joke? I had to hide my unmanly curiosity since even the girls seemed uninterested in it. I mean in the box. In fact, now I think about it, Helen probably wore a smug smile when she breathed her "Wonder what's in the box." I said, "Let's do it. I have to get more wood anyway." That's as nonchalant as I could manage.

At The Land, Jube removed screws, took my heavy-hammer and tonked the edge at the top and on all corners, and the sides fell away, revealing … some sort of … statue. "A sprite!" Helen exclaimed, as if that would be just perfect. Hannah acted as surprised as we, and, I realized later, said nothing, but Jube gave a snort and said, "Don't you woodsy people recognize a wood nymph? It guards your woods. Keeps raccoons from the corn. Tells snakes where the mice are. Keeps the swallows away from the bluebird's house. And who knows what other things it can do. It's sort of related to your hex sign on the barn, Helly."

We all just stood there, looking at it. I wondered if it was made of lead. Helen leaped into the breach of wordless wonder and declared, "We love it! It looks both mischievous and, somehow, powerful. Look at its fat tummy!" And she gave Jube an honest hug. "We'll put him in the wildflower patch. He's perfect. We'll call him 'Woody.' "

"Is it a *he*?" I ventured.

"Hey! Guys can have wild, curly hair and wear off-shoulder things, can't they? Besides, a girl can't stand out here in the dark protecting flora and fauna from evil."

"Not even with magic powers?"

"No," Helen said firmly, "I'd lie awake nights."

Woody the wood nymph, four feet tall, was set in the wildflowers about 50 feet from the woods, south of the rows of apple trees. Jube said it would weather just fine. It'd never have to be moved; it'd bring us luck.

Early Sunday morning, Hannah and Helen kissed goodbye

amid a flurry of Thank Yous and You're Welcomes, and Jube and I shook hands over his parting words "Say goodbye to Woody," ringing in the silence that always followed their departure.

We spent many minutes hitting Woody with our knuckles, trying to determine whether he had a weak spot we could worry about in our spare time. But he was solid as solid lead to us, and his smile began to make us feel as if he had a secret that he knew we'd never discover.

After a few weeks, we hardly remembered he was there, but we knew that before Jube's next visit we'd have an added chore: cut down the weeds around Woody, who, by the way, did a lousy job of keeping the deer away from the apples, if indeed that was one of his talents at all.

Where was the bump in the road we had feared not long ago? Did we go over it without noticing? Was it yet to come?

In the spring, I took off my business suit and retired from the business world. It wasn't a sudden decision. I had known when I started and looked out at 35 years of 7:30 to 6:00 that I didn't want to work one day longer than necessary. I did my job well and even liked the contributions I made, both large and small, to the success of the company and to the betterment of the world in general. But when Elizabeth and Jack had become teenagers, I had looked at the future and decided to plan for an early retirement; after their graduation from college, I announced my intentions, started the wheels turning for my replacement, and inadvertently started the wheels of rumor turning, too. People figured there must be an illness involved, or a disagreement with the company, or something unusual that would persuade a man who had a fine position to leave it to do "nothing." But we just smiled at their shocked reactions. We had nothing to hide. We loved the company I worked for. We thought its people were top notch. We had seen it grow from a "little brother" to a successful company with its own business that did not need to imitate the methods and systems its parent companies used. But to decide at age 54 that a person could live "happily ever after" without becoming president or traveling 50% of his work year—that was unheard of in the days of the early 1980s.

Helen was my chief supporter in this decision. "It's your money," she said, and she meant it. She had no desire to move to a palatial residence and serve hundred-dollar late-grape wine in hundred-dollar glasses. She had her hobbies of playing in a couple local bands, plus bridge club, tennis, writing poetry, and probably some more activities that I hadn't even noticed during my working years. And she knew that I wasn't about to hang around her like a puppy dog waiting for her to throw a stick. Her girlfriends didn't even have to ask "What are you going to *do* with a husband hanging around all day?" They had all known about our unique method of camping in Florida one winter when I had only a week to get away.

It was in March. Elizabeth and Jack were in high school. We had a big case of cabin fever. Our yard had left-over black mounds of snow waiting in 15 degrees to be covered by the annual nor'easter that would set spring back another five weeks. Four months of gray skies were making us yearn for the warm blues and greens of Florida. Our teenagers had time off after exams, but once again I could only block off five working days on my calendar. Helen remonstrated, "Grouching into Spring is not the way to greet the daffodils that innocently expect their appearance to cause great joy."

What with that encouragement, I offered a solution: "With two bags apiece, four carryons, we can fly to Florida and camp for seven days!"

Helen registered some disbelief. "All our cooking utensils?

All our sleeping bags? What about golf? Tennis? In fact, what about a tent?" It was the type of challenge I liked, so two days later I showed her my packing system: three large flight bags made for golf clubs. Take four sets of necessary golf clubs and put them in two regular golf bags. Put a canvas golf bag into the pocket and distribute the four pairs of shoes in other pockets. Use the third golf bag for all the tent and awning poles. Wrap sleeping bags around the tops and tie them. Set these into the center of the large flight bags. Zip up. Then a tent bag holds the tent, folded awning, and pillow. Three large suitcases each hold a tennis racket and pillow plus clothing. Helen's holds a sauce pan and frying pan, too. The fourth suitcase is a catch-all for the other pans, flashlights, tools, silverware, and trouble light. Pack valuables in the carryons with the essentials such as books, radio, and cards. Helen "ahem-m-md," but Elizabeth and Jack were eager to fly. We carried on only three bags, left Michigan at 4:30 p.m. on Saturday, arrived in Sarasota, folded our 6'7" Jack into the little rented car, and had the tent up on our reserved site by 11 p.m.! Eureka!

Admittedly, we used paper plates and had to buy two folding chairs and two dish pans, but we donated them to a church's flea market when we left. We also bought a two-burner Coleman stove. For the return trip, we stuffed laundry into the tent bag and thereby had room for the stove in the suitcase. We returned to Michigan ready to slush into Spring. In fact, the trip was so rewarding that two years later Helen and I packed up the gear and took a jet to Florida again. People at work surely think we're a bit crazed; in fact they've told me so by asking with incredulity, "You'd pound a stake into a hill of fire ants, bail two dishpans full of water out of the tent, read by flashlight, rather than relax in a motel and order room service?"

So now the time had come to goof-off full time. We would

not be “in each other’s way” as the well-intentioned counselors to retirees warned. Counselors seemed to scare more people about retirement than they helped, we thought. Our problem was to decide what to do first, and after that our problem was to keep it fun and not let it start to run us.

Helen was a tomboy as a young girl and she still has a bit of the hoyden in her. She likes digging in the dirt at The Land and camping in 30 degrees. So after I gave the apple trees their spring drenching, we took off on a two-month camping trip to “see the redwoods before they meet with some calamity.” We made a big circle via Banff on the top and Colorado Springs on the bottom, putting up the camper every night. We hadn’t even considered buying a trailer, yet. We broke the routine by putting on some good clothes and driving into certain cities for dinner. One city was San Francisco. The trolley cars weren’t running, so we missed its greatest tourist attraction. “Another of Hank’s Happenings,” our friends would laugh. But we didn’t really care. We’d have an excuse to return for a ride some day. For now, we were on the road, and each morning after we had folded the tent into its camper base and pointed the car west, west, west, Helen said. “You don’t have to go to work today!” and I said, “I don’t have to go to work today!” just to let it reverberate and sink in and begin to drown out the habit of going to work for 30 years. We had blue skies the entire trip—a very good omen considering my reputation of being able to make it rain anywhere, anytime. And finally came the time to turn the car east, east, east, and we headed happily out of the mountains and returned to our flatlands and our farmland. We had things to do. Not promises to keep. From now on our lives would be more influenced by the ebb and flow of growing things than by the artificial incentives of flow charts.

September. Our first berries ripen. "I like the Heritage best," Helen offered. "The Summit aren't as big. The Amity aren't as sweet and they sort of crumble. We ought to plant enough so we can share them more freely."

I agreed. "According to the *Pomona,* berries are a heck of a lot easier to take care of than apples. You just whack down the canes at the end of the season and the plants grow up from the roots the next spring, grow all summer, and produce berries again in September. That sure beats growing apples. Besides, with an apple you can never tell what might be lurking inside. There's an outfit in New Jersey that sells wholesale, and there's something called a 'Rubus Convention.' We ought to go to just to find out what's going on."

Helen replied, "We already know nobody is growing berries around here. Used to be fun to take the kids out to that place six miles from town. Can't remember the place, but it's been gone for years. And those were summer berries. Hot? Pricky? I don't really know why it was so much fun."

We went to the convention and heard enough about fruit marketing to know for certain that we didn't want to run a fruit market that sold the obligatory pencils with berries on them, and aprons with berries on them. We didn't want to have art fairs to draw people to pick berries. We sort of automatically agreed that we'd just grow berries.

I ordered 1,000 bare root (dormant) plants—"sticks" Helen says—and while we waited for their arrival, I plowed and disced and dragged and disced and dragged the field until a handful of dirt would sift nicely between my fingers. Jack came home on a spring break, so we decided to go fishing, taking the chance that the berries wouldn't arrive for a few more days. Of course, we returned to find out a big yellow semi had backed down our little court and dropped off 1,000 plants in three huge boxes. Helen had actually gone out and planted several hundred. Jack and I joined her and finished the planting in two days. The plants had white growths on them. Jack went back to school. We watched and waited, and nothing happened: nothing at all. Jack was "bummed."

The next spring the company replaced the plants but we had already lost a year's growth. "We aren't timing this, remember?" I cautioned. "A farmer is nothing if not patient and optimistic. Farming would be totally boring if we weren't dependent upon the whims of the weather and various tricks of Mother Nature." I said this. But I was anxious, too, to stand back and watch things grow. So we planted 1,000 again, and just to hedge our bets, I ordered 500 more from a company in Minnesota that specialized in berries. By midsummer we saw tiny leaves; by early August we had a few berries. *Next* September we'd have a *ton*, we imagined. Judy picked a quart. We took her picture—our first paying customer! And then that night the rains began and continued and continued until the "500 year flood" was official.

Woody grinned his foolish grin while rain dropped from his curly hair and water rose to where his belly button presumably was under the swirling robe and vines. The flood did not announce itself with great storms; it crept upon us while rain fell steadily for days. As they said, the creeks did rise and so did our drainage ditch and the feeder ditches along the road. Besides the berries being swamped, the several hundred little miniature pumpkins—the latest rage in decorative autumn accents that Helen planted for a local fruit market to sell—were drowned. The river along Main Street flowed into town; sewers backed up; homes were damaged; fields and fields of corn, beans, and beets that were near harvest became waterlogged. Our house in town was unscathed—its roof was reshingled that summer and the circling drain tiles were cleaned out. We were lucky to only lose a garden and a berry harvest. The barn floor had several inches of water, but our tools and machinery had no permanent damage. What with the crisis at hand, we hardly noticed our own loss. Besides, most of the berries would grow again next year. My miles, shovelful by shovelful, of buried drainage tiles worked well once the water level returned to normal. So we ordered 500 more plants for replacement "just in case." Besides, some expansion was justified considering the questions we'd been getting about when our berries would be ready. We had gotten calls in July. People had to be reminded that ours were a wonderful, new, autumn type of berry that one could pick in comfortable coolness and without the pests of flies and mosquitoes. Changing people's habits might take awhile, but we felt that once they got used to thinking of berries in September, they'd rejoice. It was only a new time we were introducing, not a new fruit. Then we hit the "bump in the road."

It began one balmy summer evening in 1985 when we were driving to Bay City to have one of our rare special dinners at an up-scale restaurant. Helen said, "Boy, my glasses are crooked. Those two black birds over the trees—one is really faint and almost on top of the other. Look at them over there above the birches."

"There's only one, I think," was my reply.

Helen spent the next few months adjusting glasses and trying to get the pictures on the living room wall to hang straight. "I look at them and they tilt and slide down the wall," she said. The ophthalmologist stated, "There's nothing wrong with your eye muscles." What was it, then?

In January, 1986, Helen planned to take her Mother to lunch in celebration of her 80th birthday. It was January 28, the day of the Challenger disaster. I was at the Buick dealer looking over the new models when a mechanic rushed into the showroom and said, "The shuttle … the Challenger … It blew up!" We lost interest in buying and selling, and I went home. Helen said her Mother wanted to go to lunch and that "She has a protective reflex so she doesn't let calamities affect her personally." So they met Judy at the restaurant as planned and raised wine glasses to "Happy Birthday" while the entire restaurant had no smiles visible. On that day, Helen tilted her head back while driving the car, trying to see clearly enough to get home.

That was the beginning, followed by tremors, heart palpitations, and loss of weight. Yet Helen forged ahead, intent upon beating "menopause." We followed our usual routine at The Land, and even went camping up north and took a trip to Toronto. All the while she'd complain of being really warm, but it was a hot summer and I was warm, too. The difference was my skin was not hot to touch. Finally, her doctor said, "My patients gain weight, they don't lose weight." It was almost a relief to hear the diagnosis: Graves' Disease.

Radioactive iodine "killed off my overactive thyroid," as she describes it. Then began seven months of wearing an eyepatch to avoid double vision, and five years of waiting for the gritty, painful, swollen, weepy eyes to stabilize. She played tennis and golf and continued all her favorite activities except playing her sax. Blowing made her head hurt. One day she announced, "I bet I can sing without hurting my head," and she joined Sweet Adelines and sang for three years until she announced, "I feel like Hildegarde, and they want me to jump around like Liza Minelli." Then she joined a Contemporary Christian Singers group and liked the wonderful music. But, finally, she said, "I guess I'm tired of performing. I tap-danced to 'Alexander's Ragtime Band' when I was seven years old. I've had enough."

So the bump in the road caused us to make adjustments. After two eye operations, Helen acted as if the disease never happened. Except once in a while she'll say, "I'm so ugly with these bulgy eyes. Too bad people have to look at me."

I say, "You look fine. Besides, you're a survivor."

And she says, "I survived because you helped me."

And I say, "You could have just sat down and complained but you hung in there."

And she perks up again and says, "I'm stuck in all this treacle."

During those five years, we had the crop failures, the flood, and the drought. The drought was probably hardest because it was the third time that we waited and watched as the canes and leaves grew and grew.

There was still no water source at The Land. We didn't think the drainage ditches would be a good source; besides, when we needed water, the ditches were dry. There was still no electricity either. I couldn't see the sense in having a well drilled when we didn't really have a business, even though it looked more and more like we were going to have U-PICK berries at the rate we were planting. But first the bushes had to grow and produce. So I developed a system that complemented my willingness to be outdoors and get exercise. I left the house at 8:30 a.m. with 12 five-gallon jugs of water in the back of the Chevy truck. I poured the jugs, one at a time, into watering cans and walked up and down the row, watering as I walked. By 9:30 Helen came to help pour, then she took the empty jugs back home, filled them, returned. This we did two and three times a day for several days. In this manner we kept the new plants alive. We couldn't think that the drought might continue longer than a few weeks, not after just having had "the flood of the centuries" the season before. So we hacked weeds, which never suffer from anything, and I daydreamed about a new system that would use a 250 gallon drum in the back of the pickup. The mildly damp-looking clouds drifted overhead and away day after day, so I bought a big white plastic drum, loaded it on the truck and drove home to fill it with water. Cal came from next door to see what fool thing I was doing today. He studied the big drum and said, "That's the biggest portable potty I ever saw!" "Whatever works" I said as we laughed a little. I drove slowly sloshing back to The Land. There,

Helen jumped up on the tailgate and aimed the hose while I drove between the rows. It worked. The next day I rigged up a pipe system that would let the water run out when I removed the cap. That worked better because Helen didn't have to help.

We hoed and watched for signs of new growth. I ordered 1,000 one-quart berry boxes, and we search the stores for five-quart, white pails for picking so that each customer would have both hands free to pick, the pail hanging from a belt we would provide. Information we gleaned from the bramble and rubus conferences had convinced us that having a scale would be a nuisance, what with licenses and inspections, so we decided to offer the same methods that we enjoyed ourselves, namely, filling a clean white pail half full and pouring the rubies, er, berries gently into wooden quart boxes. We also learned that black lettering on white background is the best color for signs, so Helen lettered two signs for the ends of the mile road:

U-PICK RASPBERRIES 3/4 mile (arrow)	U-PICK RASPBERRIES (arrow) 1/4 mile

She pasted black numbers on the 13 white stakes I had made for the start of each row, and we ordered a 20-foot banner for the front of the barn. Then she got artistically inspired, drawing the front of the barn (with "It's the berries!" printed on the barn door) onto 3" by 5" raspberry red cards that also stated hours, directions to the patch, and were headlined by the words AWESOME AUTUMN RASPBERRIES! YOU PICK! We intended to hand them to customers and to anyone else we'd meet who expressed an interest. So. We were definitely ready to open for business; if it would only rain.

And, lo! the rain came! The little white blossoms appeared. The bees droned. And then one day as we looked across the field from our approach along the road, we saw a slight red tint. Berries! Berries! We put an ad in the local paper. We got a few customers. Each one said "I didn't know berries grow in the fall!" Each one was thrilled. Some were reminded of their childhoods and July berries. Some remembered picking berries at Grandmother's house. Some "just love to pick berries" and gave them to elderly friends ; others wanted to "surprise bridge club with a raspberry pie." They were happy people. Helen said, "I feel as if we're doing a community service but it's much better than giving free flu shots!" And I felt that way, too. It was uplifting to see people so enthusiastic. They heard honking, so they'd stop to watch geese trying to get their misshapen X into the proper, precise arrowhead; they'd see deer tracks between the rows; they'd see raccoon tracks; they'd ask about our apples and we'd give away some early varieties. It was a party until the early killing frost.

We took down all the signs and put one up that said "Sorry. Berries frozen solid. Please call next season. Thank you." We answered the phone, commiserating with our customers' disappointment. By week's end, six inches of snow muffled the layers of crinkly leaves in the woods. On Saturday, Helen and I relaxed in our living room. I mulled over the frantic, short-lived berry season. Helen paused in her knitting of a blue afghan and said, "Hank! We didn't put any berries in our freezer!"

"How come?"

"I don't know. I guess I thought I'd wait until our customers had all they wanted. You know even after we'd close, I could glean a few quarts."

"Well," I said, "we'll just have to pretend we never heard of autumn berries."

The doorbell rang. It was Jan. She said, "Here's a quart of berries. I couldn't stand it knowing you hadn't frozen any."

"But how did you know?" Helen asked.

Jan said, "Remember I picked on Monday around noon and you close at 1:00. On Tuesday the sign was up. I figured the frost caught you."

"I can't believe it! Thank you so much!" Helen said.

"You're welcome," Jan said. "I love to pick berries. See you next year!"

Helen brought the bag of individually frozen berries to me. They looked like big rubies.

"Look," she said. "We've been given a quart of our own berries. What wonderful people come to our place! Elizabeth will have her Christmas pie after all." She put the berries in the freezer, sat down, and picked up her knitting. But she talked while she knit: "Did you read *Lady Chatterly's Lover*?"

"What?"

"Did you read *Lady Chatterly's Lover*?"

"Why do you want to know?" I asked, carefully.

"Did you?" Helen persisted.

"I don't remember."

"This Nature business reminds me of it. It's about this fine lady who has an affair with someone of lower class but there's no sex or violence or—"

"She has an affair but there's no sex?"

"Well, there is one part I remember that surprises and thrills *her* instead of the usual vice versa, but it was vital to reveal the man's character and the female's suppressed, usually, needs. But there is not purposely explicit lengthy description like the stuff being written these days; there's a lot left to the imagination which can be a lot more exciting and is a lot less embarrassing and insulting."

"I still don't remember," I said.

"Well, it doesn't matter because it's the Preface to the book that is more important anyway, and even if you had read the book, you probably wouldn't have read the Preface. The author talks about the problems of society and classes of society and why we can't get along anymore, and he says it's because we've done away with the seasonal renewals of the soul that used to bring everyone together in a sort of common rebirth and recognition of each other as frustrated mortals with the same problems. And during those celebrations we unite with the forces of Nature in which our roots lie and we become one people, and we don't have those anymore. Like true autumn harvests where entire villages get together and either weep together and support each other over a bad season or else celebrate over a good one. It's an Earth thing. No newspaper tells people when it's a holiday nor reminds them what they should do with it. He says we've lost the *rhythm* that accompanies the rise and fall of the seasons, the ebb and flow of the oceans, the moon's relation to our innermost feelings. My mother once wrote a line: "I am sister to the moon."

"What did she mean?"

"She was trying to explain that all things are connected and all have their primal source and therefore their primal power."

"Your mother could raise her and everyone else's blood pressure with stuff like that."

"I know, Hank, but it was mainly a revelation to herself, I guess. It was sort of comforting. "A sister to the moon" implies we're all in this together and we got here without asking to be born and we don't know where we're going. There's a longing people have these days to be a more intimate part of the natural pendulum as a group—high and low society, rich and poor, all classes, all colors—instead of just a separate, cold creature at the mercy of, say, the roll of the dice. Today people want to be unique and separate. They splinter into groups of their own kind, quarrel over imagined insults. They don't realize that all people can blend into one unit—humanity—and work together but still be individuals with their own heritage. The Preface said Man has both a deep and a shallow need and neither should be ignored."

"What's the deep need?" I asked, though I felt this was getting deep itself.

"That Oneness I was just telling you about. That physical moon/earth/seasons thing. Stonehenge effect—witnessing the sun's rays in relation to you. Indians blessing creatures. And then you can also add on all the games, the humor, the sharing of different customs and celebrations, the daily not the seasonal nourishment—like the way bear cubs tumble in the snow just for the delight. It asks if mankind really prefers absolute independence of women and state support of motherhood, and if so, women might choose never to have babies, and if they do have babies, never to stay home and nurture them. And if that happens mankind will be thrust even further into the gloom of frustration because men won't have anyone to provide for and women won't have nurturing and everyone will be for the individual and not for humankind."

"And *that* was banned in Boston?"

"You *did* read it!" Helen exclaimed.

"I remember the title now. Helly, let's have some popcorn. You make the popcorn and I'll fix some drinks and I'll build a fire. Let's celebrate the end of our first berry season."

Helen said that was a marvelous idea. We got a couple pillows, propped them on the floor against the front of the couch and settled down for a fine evening of light conversation in front of a flickering fire.

But Helen was not to be sidetracked from her evening's machinations.

"So what do you think about all that I said?" Helen asked. She expected a thoughtful answer, as usual, so I tried to sound as if I had been very attentive.

"About what?" I had to ask.

"About Nature and seasons and nurturing and everything," she said, helpfully.

"I'm not sure about all that moon stuff, but I sure do like being outside and watching and waiting for things to grow and having melons in season, and tomatoes in season, and your homemade applesauce, and talking like a farmer with our real farmer who is as happy as I am when our little crops grow well. I'm happy when he has a good soybean harvest. Yeah, I think civilization is missing something. There sure is a lot of boredom and general dissatisfaction and frustration out there these days."

"That's why I'm really ticked off at Joseph Campbell."

I asked, "What did poor Joe do?"

"He spent years and years teaching and writing about the relationships and similarities among all the myths of the world," Helen said. As if that cleared things up.

"Greek and Roman gods that do dumb things and have unpronounceable names."

"Joe, as you call him, said myths are clues to our deepest spiritual potential—when we just can't help dancing with the rapture of being alive. But the modern world of technology and separation has destroyed belief in the myths, so we've lost what molded us when one part of the world didn't even know that there was another part somewhere. Now as the world is made small with instant communications, we have factions that kill those who don't agree with their ideas. All the myths have a common thread that should bind all humanity together instead of splintering it. So he says we need a new mythology to give direction to this new world, so each can again find his "bliss." And the new myth probably should be the type that looks forward, gives a goal, instead of trying to explain what happened in the past, because science has pretty well explained that."

"Okay. What's the new myth?"

Helen stood up. "That's just it! There isn't any. He knew more about myths than any human being but didn't write one."

"Why don't you write one?" I suggested, half seriously.

"Good grief. You can't just conjure up something. There has to be a take-off event. Like, you know, a celestial occurrence that scares even the scientists, or the arrival of a Jesus. So he could be explained."

"Isn't the regular Jesus good enough anymore?"

"Hank, you said yourself that somebody killed The Reasonable Man, and even Emerson said, 'In Christendom, where is the Christian?' Annihilations are like rain, falling on people somewhere every day. Remember that view taken from the moon? The picture of our round, fragile Earth surrounded by blackness? Our knees got weak when we saw it Christmas Eve. It was like a heavenly message. There were no political or any other boundaries on it—just the blues and greens of rivers, mountains making one pattern of a natural whole. That view, Campbell said, could be the start of a new mythology that would be universal instead of "just for Christians, or just for Moslems etc." Even Star Wars tried to promote "good emotions over bad brains," but people were merely entertained. Who took, May The Force Be With You seriously? Earthlings are growing even tinier as other galaxies are discovered. People will develop bad neuroses as their importance in the universe shrinks and shrinks and religions will be scurrying to give people something that makes sense."

"Well, what's the answer?" I asked. I hoped she had one. I certainly didn't.

"I want everyone to be decent and happy, and maybe a new myth would give people a solid base again. I wanted Campbell to present it to us all completed, but instead we got 50 years of Freud and his suppressed sexual urges telling us 'I'm Not O.K. and You're Not Either But It's Not Our Fault' stuff."

"But what about old id and the subconscious that were his scientific discoveries?"

"Honestly! The man interpreted his own dreams and wrote up their meanings! His discoveries required a lot less subjectivity to be pure science. Society would have been more stable without Freud and with, say, Alf Wight instead. I don't know what the answer is. We're supposed to be more civilized than 3,000 years ago, but actually we've just found more subtle ways to be very mean and ugly."

"Helly, you get that old Puritan-punishment mode going and we won't be able to enjoy the Good Life. We've had our share of bad stuff. Jack's convulsions, for instance. We had to let him play and not show how worried we were. And your Graves' Disease. Now you look around for bad things in the world when we should just be grateful. You know that prayer that drives you crazy? That one that thanks God for the food we are about to receive and then asks God to make us grateful? And you always mumble to me that if God has to make us grateful for what he gives us, there's a flaw in the make-up of Man? Remember? Let's get off this heavy stuff. Mankind is saved one at a time and we've done our part." I got up, refreshed our drinks, and we each sat again in our usual place.

"It's depressing," Helen said.

"Think about that German garden book. That's one that's cheerful, you said."

"You mean Elizabeth of German Garden fame. That's a good book, I admit. Mom was born one year after its England publication, and I remember she said she used her money that she earned as a bookkeeper to buy books and piano music, things no one else in town spent money on. And she taught herself piano and, by reading, to love words. She loved that book. And *Anthony Adverse* was another. There's a grand wittiness in Garden. The author calls her husband 'the man of wrath,' and her children she refers to by the months they were born in instead of their names, so she says 'April baby did so and so.' You know she wrote over 20 books, and now they're being rediscovered and published again probably because someone decided she was a Feminist. She certainly views men as being some sort of puffed-up silliness. Her heroine's attempt at independence and recognition in *The Pastor's Wife* is exciting, sad, and humorous. But Feminists can't take all the credit for today's Woman; few of them could afford to be away from their children if antibiotics and inoculations hadn't come along to free up the mothers. Do you realize how many weeks a mother of five would be home nursing her children over whooping cough, measles, mumps, and all the various bacteria-caused illnesses before science and medicine opened the doors to let women leave the house? Still, Elizabeth's books are full of appreciation of nature and of the foibles of mankind. You ought to read one of them, at least."

"I thought you said they were women's books."

"I thought I said that they're written from a woman's viewpoint. It wouldn't hurt men to see the world through the eyes of a woman. After all, I liked *Hunt For Red October.* Of course after that Clancy got too macho-crazed."

"So you found an author who doesn't insist that God is only found among people?"

"That's part of her humor. She's always with people and trying not to be. I ordered all her books and I'm going to space them between some of the junk you pick up at sales."

"Hey, I found *Trustee In A Toolroom*," I replied.

"Okay, I admit that you do manage to find gems once in a while. But now that I've thought about it, I do think you ought to read Elizabeth. Books lack real wit and subtle humor these days. Of course, I can always conjure up that time we almost killed off our neighbors if I want a good laugh."

"Now that you've recovered from the Literary Doldrums and Despondencies, how about a walk in the woods where we can, er, admire nature."

Helen repeated, "I said, that time we almost killed off our neighbors!"

"I heard."

"When we were baby-sitting their scruffy little dog. I could get hysterical all over again."

"It was a long time ago," I insisted. I thought, "Please, no hysterics again!"

"But the timing! Jack went over and fed the dog and came back home, but then I looked out and I saw … wait a minute. I wrote a 4-S (that stands for short, short, short story) about it. I'll get it."

Helen came back waving papers at me. What could I do? I read:

What Are The Odds?

We four involved in the escapade would have said the odds are a zillion to nil, nada, null, zero, that dog-sitting could result in a police action. For one thing, the dog was a scruffy little poodle with an obnoxious-looking skin disease that kept all of us neighbors from petting her; nevertheless, our son was asked to dog-sit: "Just come over and fill her dishes with food and water every evening. Patti doesn't need to be walked—she'll use the papers we've spread in the basement." So on Thursday evening, about 7 P.M., Jack went across the street, unlocked the front door, and filled Patti-the-Poodle's dish. He returned to say she didn't act hungry, didn't even sniff the food.

Our house sits the long way on our quiet court of eight families; the house with the dog is across the street, catty-cornered, so when I passed our sliding, side door I glanced across at their kitchen. "Did you leave their light on, Jack?" I asked.

"It was on when I got there so I left it. Maybe Patti is afraid of the dark."

"Could be," I said.

My mother, who lived with us during winter months, had the Scrabble game set up on the kitchen table, so I sat down and drew my seven letters and we went at it as we did every night. Toward the end of the game, I waited 10 minutes for her to make a word. We never timed each other and we used the dictionary at will. So I got up to get a Pepsi and to close the curtains covering the sliding door. I looked at the lighted kitchen window and saw movement. "Jack! I just saw a shadow of a person walking past Stern's window."

"I'll go over and check. Patti isn't supposed to jump up there where the flowers are."

"Be careful. Things happen, you know." I really was more curious than worried. Jack returned before Mom had her word placed, and reported that everything was okay and that Patti was curled up on her rug.

An hour passed. Mom and I had finished one game when she said, "Shall we go look out the door now so we can start another game?" I knew she meant that I should have it over with, so I glanced out at the window and could barely contain myself: "It's there again, Jack."

"Mom, I was just over there."

"That was at least an hour ago," I replied, with my best you've-got-a-job-to-do voice.

My husband Hank, calm as usual, said, "I'll go over with Jack." I had the feeling he would have added, "and put a proper end to this nonsense." I said, "I'm going to phone you over there and make sure you're okay and if there's trouble, say some message like 'What time is it' and I'll get help."

When I phoned, Jack answered and said they're fine. I said, "Put Dad on the phone." Hank answered, "No, nobody has a gun to my head." So they locked the door and came home.

Mom and I finished our games by 11:30, and I couldn't resist taking one more look if only so I could go to sleep believing I'd indeed been "seeing things." This time I yelled, "It's there!" which caused Jack and Hank to get out of bed and join me at the door. Sure enough, they saw the shadow crossing the window. "Better call the police," Hank said.

"Why me?" I said.

"Just tell them we're dog-sitting for the neighbors and we think someone's in their house." He and Jack put on their clothes.

Headlights out on their patrol car, two policemen drove slowly down our court and stopped at our driveway where Hank had been waiting for them. He gave them the key, pointed at the lighted window, and retreated indoors. The policemen got out of their car, drew their pistols and began to sneak around Stern's house. We all watched from our door, not saying a word to each other. I held tight to Mom's arm.

The knock at our front door jumped us—it was the taller policeman who, while returning the key, said, "There's just an old couple sitting in the livingroom, reading."

"But my son and husband went over there three times and nobody was there!"

"Well, they live there and they're there."

The policeman tried to ease Jack and Hank's mortification, saying that most of their break-ins are reported by good, watchful, neighbors. "The Mortified" crept quietly back to bed but Mom and I released our tensions with hysterical laughter: "Three times! Three times! the Sterns left their house! And got into their Ford and drove away to do errands! And passed the blind, narrow side of our ranch house, and each time they were away, Jack and Hank slipped into the vacated house! And came out again before the Sterns got back! What are the odds?!"

We finally went to our separate bedrooms on each end of the house. I listened to the quiet for a minute and then heard Mom's giggle which started me up again so I got up and met Mom in the kitchen where we laughed tears. At 12:30 a.m., Elizabeth came home from her date and, looking first at Grandma and then at me and seeing our exhaustion, asked, "Anything happen here tonight?" We barely had enough breath to give her our fragmented recital, and though she joined us in our renewed laughs, her face looked so bewildered I knew we'd have to try again tomorrow to get through the explanation of the evening's events.

Early the next morning, Mildred Stern phoned and asked me if I knew anything about the two policemen who showed up at her door at midnight asking all kinds of questions about an intruder. They had told her, "A neighbor reported seeing activity." I admitted our gaffe. And I apologized best I could what with a giggle coming up. She said, "We're leaving on our trip now. Will Jack feed Patti as originally planned?"

"Oh, certainly," I said.

Mildred and Mike Stern left on their trip at 9 a.m.—the date we later noticed had been correctly marked on our calendar all along: Today. Friday. Not yesterday.

Odds being what they are, we don't buy lottery tickets. We'd surely win $10 million and ruin our lives.

"Helly, it wasn't that funny," I said, "it was damned embarrassing."

"Ah, the male ego. Well, maybe something funnier will happen some day. And leaving a pail of smelt in the trunk for five days doesn't qualify."

"But *that's* funny!"

"Even if you were the dolt who did it?"

"Steve and I still laugh. Couldn't figure out where the smell was coming from."

Helen used her fake-exasperation tone. "Men! Lord, even their sense of humor is different. I don't know how we ever manage to get along at all."

That sounded like a hint to me, so I said, "Now that you're *really* over your Literary Doldrums and Despondency, at my expense, how about we Puritans go out into the woods. You know, like those bear cubs. Woody can stand guard."

"But there's snow! I'd have my long johns on!" Helen said.

"I'll bring the army blanket," I said.

Helen glanced at the window, bright with the full moon on the snow. She smiled at me.

I brought two army blankets.

March came, and we hit a sort of depression, a pitfall in the getting older business, I suppose. Sure, we made lots of fun together. We'd had, so far, a good life, had felt lucky, blessed, even. But something was happening on the fringes again—like a sinister face peering over the white-washed fence we had carefully built around our lives.

Woody had been standing there for five years now, through rain, sleet, snow, sun, and the long hours and hours of twilights and deep darkness and the first pinkness of over 1,800 dawns silhouetting the treetops. Squirrels crawled on him. Sparrows sat on his curly head. The creases in his robe held mosses. More and more he looked as if he belonged there. Helen and I walked out to him to cut down some thistles.

Helen announced, "We should plant a lilac bush next to Woody."

"Why a lilac bush?"

"So years from now people would know someone was here because lilacs have to be planted. Wherever you see one, you know a farm or people once were there."

"Wouldn't Woody be a clue?"

"He'll be smashed or stolen by then. Hey! What's this shiny spot on his forehead?"

"Well, he faces north," I said. "He takes the sleet right in his face. But south, he'd get the full sun, and east he'd be looking at the woods."

"Well, we aren't going to move him. The forehead isn't too bad. It's actually sort of pretty. Not so dull. Looks like bronze."

"He's heavy enough, but it's probably some welded metal. Bronze would have cost a fortune and we'd have needed a front-end loader."

Helen asked, "Should we plaster over it or something before it gets worse? What will Jube say?"

"We'll just hang some moss and grapevines down his face and he'll never notice."

Helen laughed.

"What?"

"Jube with moss and grapevines! Ha-a-a-a."

We came home with smiles that belied our feelings.

On Sunday, no football was scheduled, no distraction. Helen was on her knees tying fringes to a fanciful afghan spread out on the floor. She made it for our grandchildren so they "wouldn't wreck Elizabeth's good one." I stared at my book. I was thinking that the more we got involved with The Land, the more The World spun away from us.

In subtle ways, we oldsters are eased out of the action. First comes the use of fad language. That doesn't bother us because each generation wants its own unique identity and we still have our own language ("the whole shebang"). But after that comes new entertainment under the guise of freedom of expression. Plato, we've been told over and over, criticized the next generation in his day, as has every older generation that is being shoved aside. But no generation has gone as far as this one of baby boomers and their offspring. "Three Dog Night" was the last name of a band that we could comprehend, which means we don't comprehend hundreds of groups calling themselves, say, the "Dead Milkmen" or "Soup Dragons." Nor do we understand the celebrities who scream and flail over a thumping amplifying system that breaks plaster and eardrums. The young audiences give these drugged performers megabucks. And the performers die from their success.

We watch "The Graduate" spin off new kinds of movies that develop themes based on shock value disguised as "reflecting society." We know they reflect society's aberrations, not society's mainstream. We elect not to go to the movies, but then the same freedom of expression comes into our house, into our living room via TV. The producers do not consider that TV by its very nature is more personal than a book or radio, that illusion becomes reality, and that they should therefore not drown us with expletives of the most vulgar type and graphic sex scenes and graphic murders. But how can we expect good judgment from an industry that proudly proclaims, "This program was filmed before a *live audience*!" They evidently consider that better than a dead one.

TV used to be tastefully or sometimes outrageously funny—a substitute for Jack Benny or Fibber and Mollie: sometimes corny, sometimes dull, but never embarrassing. We would fuss with aerials, test malfunctioning tubes at a nearby store and usually end up buying new tubes. Then came solid-state: "Do not remove back cover of set!" Color came, too. And TV became a sort of god-in-a-box. Our laughter died. So laugh tracks replaced us. Body-parts language infested all the media, wounding the noble spirit of user and hearer. Then satellite dishes caught every hostile act from every tiny part of the planet Earth—a school bus went off a road on Santa Cruz and we, in our town in Michigan, mourned the deaths of the children. "No man is an island" is accurate and important, and we must take care of each other, but we cannot withstand bombardment, that emotional drain that takes away from us the very vitality that would make us caring and helpful persons. TV was no fun anymore.

We hoped they'd at least leave our cowboy movies alone. But no. "Silverado" is billed as a marvelous western, but it actually is "Miami Vice" moved west. There must have been at least 25 deaths in that movie, whereas the old classic "Red River" showed one poor cowboy meet with swift death, which was followed by his sad funeral. The dead in "Silverado" must still be lying there, unmourned.

Then, there's the school: no island where teachers are able to spend their time uplifting, expanding, increasing thirst for knowledge. Parents go to work, both of them. They give latchkeys to their children but forget about the keys used for coping. The parents become irritable, being torn by work and home and kids, so they turn to the schools and receive for their children breakfasts; after-school lodging, entertainment, and snacks; counseling; health care; sex education; drug information; decision-making skills; family life courses. And the schools promise not to wound the egos of these children. Schools will not inform the children that the world is a tough place full of tough competition and they'd better work their butts off if they want to amount to something. Parents get burned out and divorce. Teachers get burned out and quit. Helen and my married-two-kids-dog family becomes the dysfunctional family in this society. One-parent families hold sway. These groups demand innumerable supports from society, and no one may say to them that theirs is not the proper road to take. Compared to all this, Jean Valjean slogging through a sewer with the soldier on his back seems a simple act that fixes wide-ranging problems.

Of course, as we are being eased out of the decisions, we are required to be sure to send our money to the state, the schools, the Feds and all the feeder arms so that society can continue in the direction that it has decided to take. We watch The World with its political correctness terrified to call a spade a spade. It is as foreign to us as a kapok tree but without any of the tree's beauty. So okay we say, when our end is near, we will go out onto the ice floe and quietly drift away. But no, they say. Here, they say, take a gun. We've got plenty to spare. It's easy. You just pull the trigger. We do it all the time. It gets us anything we want. I say, But it's wrong. They say, Wrong? Wrong is poverty, being alone, being unloved, being ignored. But having a gun is having it all. I say I'll make a deal: you give me your guns, and I'll give you this helmet. They say, Helmet? Oh, I get it! Virtual Reality! Yeah, I say. You go into this building. There are enough rooms to keep you entertained for the rest of your life. I'll send your friends to you when they give me their guns. You'll be in high-tech heaven with all the electronic cadavers you can take apart, or you can fish under the ice or travel inside a brain or do almost anything that gives you your high, and you can do it right here … .

Helen draped the afghan over my chest. I opened my eyes.

"Well, Mr. Hilarious, where have you been daydreaming?" she asked.

"We're getting old, Helly."

Helen retorted, "Nonsense. You haven't shrunk, have you?"

"Er … ."

"You're still 6'2-1/2". You've still got most of your hair, and some of it is beginning to look like my lovely white curly tresses. You've got your same sparky olive eyes."

"They're brown."

"Only on your driver's license," Helen said. "It must be time to get out the seed catalogs or go fishing. Didn't Jack sound like he needed a break, too, after IBM lost that bid? You said it must be hard to have two years' work go down the tubes. And he's always interested, in fact downright enthusiastic, about getting out of the beltway hassle for awhile. If he could get away, I bet you could meet somewhere. Somewhere warm. You need to quit reading the liberal papers awhile and get back in touch with all the good people out there. You know, in all the jillions of miles we've traveled, we've gotten ripped off just that one time when our oars were swiped in that national forest way back when Elizabeth was, what, ten maybe. Anyway, I've got stuff I can do here, and you can go visit your sisters on the way. Talk about good people! And they're older than we are and are having a ball, and you hardly see them."

"I'd like to see what all the hoopla is about in Cancun."

"And get drowned trying to snorkel off a boat in high seas again?"

"If it's rocky, we won't go out," I promised.

"Is that related to 'If the weather is bad, we won't continue over the ice,' and 'The tornado is heading northeast so it'll miss us by a couple miles'? Actually, I'd rather go there when we can plan it and anticipate it. Now you could just go and fish and by the time you come back it'll almost be like spring."

Jack just had to get his plane tickets. I just had to load up the truck. Saved again.

A big, yellow truck delivered new high-tech berry plants in early June after, with luck, all danger of frost had passed. I had ordered 250 of them after reading about propagation by tissue culture. The method guaranteed exact duplication of the mother plant that was selected for the correct variety, being free of disease, hardy, and all the good stuff one looked for in a plant. If we were amazed, we could always order more.

Each little plant already had three leaves, like delicate strawberry plants. What a sight compared with the thousands of sticks we were used to planting. So we planted, watered, and watched. They grew and grew. We would surely get an early start on this season. But they grew and grew and never produced a berry! They didn't look at all like our Heritage variety, because they weren't! Our red-faced supplier, of course, would replace them next spring. Helen wrote to *Pomona* asking whether anyone else had been unhappy with a tissue-culture experiment. We expected to get a dozen replies, at least, or maybe three or four. But we got not a letter. Nor was any comment printed in the next issues. It was eerie. Were we the only ones who had ventured into the high-tech arena? Whatever the reason, we would have to plant 250 plants again next spring. That is, if "the creek don't rise" again.

A Fistful of Flowers

Ben is running up my garden path.
A little girl used to hurry like that, too,
excitement stumbling her carefree toddler-run:
Across the grass she bobbled, then up the porch,
one foot, other foot, one foot, other foot;
an urgent pounding on the door—her fist
still holding strangled dandelions
she had picked especially for me.

Now Benjamin is running up the path,
holding a bouncing bunch of yellow—no, blue
bedraggled flowers he's found beneath the hedge.
> *I remember finding a violet there*
> *when pulling weeds. It was a cool May day,*
> *the kind that lures me with its promises.*
> *I trimmed the lilac, clipped cotoneasters,*
> *filled the birdbath with unfeathered water,*
> *and there! One hello violet! pretending*
> *to be fragile, alone, but soon enough*
> *outgrowing clover and forget-me-nots.*
> *Who first called you shy? shrinking? Your leaves*
> *have all the heart of wildflower pioneers*
> *forever moving west, sending scouts*
> *ahead to stake new claims upon my lawn,*
> *dappling it with little violet flags …*

"Grama! S'prise!" Ben jumps into my arms,
(his eyes are blue as violets!)
giving my cheek his wet, wide-Mason-jar kiss.

The old glass vase is perfect—Ben's bouquet
hangs limply over the rim, like dandelions.

Sometime between the removal of 3/4 of the apple trees and the planting of the tissue culture berries we were presented with 1) a grandchild 2) Jube's disappearance—the first event happily anticipated; the second, quite a surprise.

A grandchild! Love enveloped the child long before he was born. Helen rose to poetic heights: "Both sets of grandparents, all the brothers and sisters and cousins of the expectant parents, all prepared a mental and emotional lovenet to welcome this new soul, this new spirit from another plane of existence into our strange mortal world that we were presently experiencing albeit from varying heights of age and observation." My thoughts, exactly.

Elizabeth and Brad are both first-born children so, psychologists say, they have above average doses of grit. But whatever "first, middle, or last child" influences might have had, it is true that they are mature young people. After college and marriage, Elizabeth worked while Brad earned an MBA and learned to prepare dinners. There were walking-on-thin-ice months during the pregnancy until Brad found a job. Then, at the height of normal married-life expenses, they began to repay college loans and send monthly support to a destitute child in the Philippines. A baby in their home would be a lucky baby indeed, because he'd have discipline, love, humor, companionship, and the close ties of a caring church family. Knowing this, our years of the empty nest were more like years of watching their progress from some majestic tree that they had left confidently.

The old "amount to something" certainly was evident in these children of ours, and we were very grateful to Whatever for sparing us pain. We felt that our luck, and/or Whatever, would continue to bless our grandchild; yet "grandchild" was still a scary thought, and Helen had mixed feelings of concern and happiness for our daughter. After all, Helen knew about birthings, whereas

I merely splutter inanities of relief. But dear Gordon came into Elizabeth and Brad's life as if it were quite a natural thing to do: Jack hurried from grad school to hold and behold his first nephew. He held him as Helen looked over his shoulder at this two-day old infant in her son's arms, and baby Gordon opened his eyes and they were large, and royal blue, and had long lashes, and they calmly pierced Jack and Helen's hearts, saying, "Here I am. I understand everything. Don't worry." Helen and Jack never will recover from that thunderbolt.

We thought it was a risky venture to bring children into today's violent world, but of course, after entertaining thoughts like that for a millisecond, we realized that we had had our babies because of love. We did not consult the latest demographic charts, nor heed the Think Tanks' warnings about overpopulation, nor all the other sophisticated alerts about humankind's survival. After all, we had miraculously escaped the polio epidemic; survived all the childhood diseases for which there were no inoculations; lived through the Depression, WWII, Korean Conflict and experts' warnings that we all should prepare a stocked bomb shelter and ask ourselves if we'd share our hoard with an unwise neighbor or friend; we'd survived the Cold War that threatened annihilation. The Berlin Wall went up, and, miracle of miracles, came down during our lifetime; Americans walked upon the moon. Upon the moon! All the events tend to take the hysteria out of the doomsayers' warnings. We knew that if the world was to have any chance of becoming a better world, people like our children should have children.

What's more, the climate of prediction now has swung its pendulum to the other extreme, so the year 2020—or "MMXX" insists Helen, observer of copyrights and inscriptions—is going to be a doozy. Illegal drugs will be so disdained that rare users will be shunned; all schools will be equally high-tech with adequate financing; the environment will be as pure as the forest where Snow White danced with chirping bluebirds; all the endangered species will be off the list; the tropical rain forest will be saved; unmarried teenagers will not have babies for society to raise; crime will be an unfeared statistic; we'll all eat only those foods that The State mandates are essential to live to 102; we'll "Bonjour" our neighbors every morning at 6:30 when beginning our two-mile jogs; nobody will drive drunk; and, best of all, the crime of the puritanical century—cigarette smoking—will have just evaporated into clean air. Surely, at least by MMXX! May Helen and I live to see it! Red Skelton's wistful goodbye said it best: May God Bless.

As usually happens when we take a breath of rarefied air, we noticed our parachute was a bit entangled in our lines of thought. This time we untangled each other in time to open a package Helen got.

Helen said, "It's from Hawaii! It's a weedy bird with a grassy nest on its back."

"Who do we know in Hawaii?"

"I don't know. Here's a note: 'The only thing I could find not made in Japan. Love, Hannah.' I didn't know they were going to Hawaii, did you?"

I suggested, "Maybe Jube finally agreed to take his wife on one of his trips."

"It could be an Easter basket," Helen guessed.

"Why would a bird have a nest on its back?"

"It's like a planter. Or a candy dish. Anyway, it was nice of Hannah to send me something. And it is unusual. She knows I won't find one at the corner store. I wonder how long they're staying."

"Probably as long as it takes Jube to find a deal."

"There's no address. No phone number. Just have to wait, I guess."

It was a month or more later, the end of July maybe, before Helen got a note. She came out to The Land with it, and read it to me. I leaned on the hoe and wished I'd gotten a drink of water before she started in.

Helen was clearly excited. "Listen to this! 'Hope your garden is growing and blah … blah … blah … I've fallen in love with the islands. Jube is off to Malaysia—gone two weeks already—and I'm having a ball! You should see the deserted beaches this time of year but nice and hot. It's my kind of life!! Am learning a new basket trick to show you. John is nicely tanned (he's the teacher) and is trying to convince me to stay all year but we haven't sold the business yet. God! I wish those three Japanese would bite! Anyways, I'm ready! Love … .' "

"That doesn't say much."

"Yes and no."

"You mean that part about that Jim teacher?"

Helen replied, "Gym teacher? He's a basket teacher. John."

"Yeah. John. Just another hobby. She's good at hobbies. Could make a living with her hobbies."

"But, Hank, she doesn't write 'ha-ha.' "

"Let me see."

I read the note twice. Seeing the words without the "ha-ha" after "stay all year" did seem out of character, but the exclamation marks all over the place were normal. So that's what I said to Helen.

"But she's my sister!"

"Remember your pledge, Helly! A long time ago we agreed that people make their own decisions that affect their own lives, remember? You can't change people. Need I mention your mother's wanting a house and picket fence and everyone coming over for her Sunday dinner? And remember when Nick didn't know what to do with his life? How many years did you stew over them?"

Helen sighed. "I know. I know," she said.

"Besides, there's no return address. No date, even. You'll have to use ESP again."

"Not funny."

"Well, I gotta finish this row. I don't see anything to get excited about."

"But I don't like the sound of it. Jube and Hannah always are together."

"Helly, Jube's been gone half their married life! You know that as well as I do. Hell! These darn horsetail weeds go on forever!"

"Aren't they mare's tails?"

"Whatever," I said. "I'm going to have to find something that isn't banned to kill 'em. Helly, I hate to see you get all wrapped up in something that drains you while the people you're concerned about go happily along. What are you going to do?"

"Nothing. What choice do I have?"

Funny how she has to worry when there's nothing she can do about it. She says she's not worrying, says she's just thinking and preparing for all the alternatives that could occur. And she hates me to call her a worrywart. Women have different minds, all right. She wants me to say, "I know you're concerned. I'm concerned too. We'll get through this together." The trouble is, I'm not concerned and she knows it. And she knows I do more thinking than talking. Maybe she feels less needed these days, too. Maybe I should tell her that she's still 5'8" and has a wonderful smile. Maybe we both feel we're pushing our luck. Maybe she *did* ward off the evil hobgoblins all these years and it wasn't really just luck. Thus I tortured myself while whacking weeds, and the damn weeds added their own torture making my shoulders ache and putting the fear of debilitating arthritis in my head.

That night I didn't bring the Hannah subject up at all. I had planned to after "Jeopardy!" but since Helen seemed to have put it aside, I figured, why should I haul it out.

Six weeks later, Helen's startled "Hannah!" into the phone got me off the chair, and I picked up the phone in the bedroom. Hannah was talking fast:

"This is hard, Helly, hard to tell you so I'll just tell you. Jube never came back to Hawaii. I'm home. The business is sold. I'm going back to Hawaii."

"You're going back? Alone? Where's Jube?"

"Helly, I should have listened better. When he left he said something about retiring in Hawaii. Yesterday I went through his metal box and found the title to a place there. It's the one we were staying in. I think … he planned to disappear."

"I don't believe this! Did you call the police? Hannah? Hannah?"

"I can't. He left a sort of explanation. You know the cops hate marital disputes, and this isn't even one."

"But aren't you worried?"

"It's weird. Jube had all our investments and finances in perfect order and set me up, and I just think, I don't know, I just think he sort of eased himself out of our life."

"We'll come over, Hannah. Don't go until we can talk."

"It's a 1930s bungalow on Diamond Head, board and batten, and termites. John knows what's got to be done to fix it. And I'll move in September."

"But that's berry season!"

"I knew you'd say that! But, Helly, I can't stay here. It's been sold. And I *want* to go. It's warm. And you really can't understand all this, I know. But give it some time and you'll see that it isn't so out of character as you think. You didn't really know Jube except when we were all together celebrating for being together and on our best behavior and, well, you'll see that I'm really okay and I really have to get going now."

"Look, Hannah, you're in shock right now."

"*You're* in shock, Helly. I'm fine. It took me awhile, but it all adds up. Why don't you two come to Hawaii after you close up? And I'll call you. I will. Don't worry."

"Fat chance," I thought, after Helen hung up with repeated exclamations of "I knew it!" Worry she did but within a maze of unanswerable questions. The main question she kept saying out loud was, "How come Hannah was so darn calm?" Helen heard a tone of fate, or resignation, in Hannah's recitation that only a sister could identify from under all the shocked surprise she herself had felt. There was, Helen thought, even a suggestion of acceptance and, my god, relief.

Frankly I was glad the second shoe had fallen so we could get on with our season. Preparations were always fun, and the "U-Pickers" brought with them an air of celebration. All indications pointed to a banner harvest. Even Helen's wildflower patch around the ginkgo tree looked like it'd honor us with profuse bloom by September instead of stubbornly staying closed until October when pickers were mostly repeats who came for a last "few more quarts for the freezer."

Woody was in his usual fine fettle. People couldn't resist saying "hello" by running their palm across his curly forehead and down his dimpled cheek, making the worn spot shinier and shinier but bringing them luck, they insisted, in whatever secret area of their lives they needed it. Who am I to question magic? Helen has thrown many a penny into a fountain, had the kids wish on a first star and over birthday candles. Every little bit helps, makes the world go more merrily around. For all I know, acts that "help thou my unbelief" might be the mental energy that actually propels old Earth. I admit I haven't patted Woody, but some mornings when I come out here at 7:30 and startle the heron up from the ditch and see the big prints of the deer that go straight across the garden, I stop and say, “Well, Woody, what happened here last night?” I think I say it, anyway. Or maybe I just think it and wish he could answer. At least Patch used to wag his body with delight and give me a clue about his feelings for the place. Woody is inscrutable. It’s annoying sometimes.

It’s even more annoying to realize nothing, absolutely nothing happened here the night before except that the Whatever was here making the grass grow, the weeds grow, the apple buds swell, the vines twine—and that’s scary enough.

Sometimes Helen feels that Life Force of Growth or Whatever that is so strong out here. She stands up from planting a sunflower seed and asks, “Why doesn’t it become a pumpkin?” Then she answers herself, “Because IT is in there.” She got mad when she finally read her mother’s favorite *Anthony Adverse*: “The entire big, fat, book is mainly his search for the meaning of life. He has tons of adventures worldwide in the early 1800s when the world’s adventures were truly basic like sailing to Africa and living there, and when he does have a very tragic happening—his wife and child die in a fire—he goes off into America’s western wilderness and lives for three years with nature, trying to find God. But he decides God is only found among people, no matter how impressive nature is. Jean Valjean of *Les Miserables* came to the same conclusion and hauled his young soldier through the putrid sewer. Are we supposed to beat the bushes to flush out and entice the needy? Jesus just accidentally met the woman at the well and all the others; he didn’t run around knocking on doors. Why should we feel guilty because we’ve chosen a simple life? We donate. We’re nice. Maybe the misery of the masses is what influenced those authors; but then, look at Lindbergh. Could the effects of the Depression cause the media and the people to devour him and then pick their teeth in satisfaction? And Hamilton said to Jefferson, or to Jackson, ‘Sir, your people is a great beast' because he didn't trust them when they act en masse, when wisdom stays out of their whirlwind. I think Anthony was wrong, and I think Candide can hoe his garden without rebuke and that God accepts people one at a time. One-on-one. Then, if a person feels moved to help others, go for it, but don't think God wasn't in the lonely garden."

I told her I didn't feel guilty and since I wasn't a great author I didn't have to deal with those questions, and that people who are kind to nature are also kind to people because there's a great amount of patience and respect involved. And I told her she could plant the corn when she was done with the sunflowers. Sweating slows down the mind.

The berry season turned out to be the banner year we had suspected it might be. But after the frantic weeks, we welcomed the hard frost that enabled us to take down the signs and reclaim our property as private once again. I began to think about where we would go for our "end-of-season celebration." One year it was Germany. Once it was England and the mesmerizing Herriot Country. I could go there again tomorrow: riding the rails in Yorkshire, buying a tea set in Oxford, and redoing London. Maybe this year we'd just opt for the trailer again and the woods up north. I actually found myself hoping that Helen wasn't worried enough about Hannah to insist we go to Hawaii. I liked Japan and Brazil when I had business there in my other life, but they are "Z" on Helen's alphabetical list of places to see. Too far, she insists.

Jack phoned, said he could meet us in the pretty hills of Pennsylvania for a weekend of autumn camping. That settled everything. We see Jack only at Christmastime unless we all make an effort to meet at some destination that is often decided at the last minute whenever he sees a break in his business calendar. So, responding to that deep motherhood urge that needs reassurance through hugs and looking into the eyes of our children, Helen gave not one thought to Hawaii. After all, Hannah certainly was not panicking; she hadn't phoned since summer.

All this reminiscing! The chair will be unable to spring back from my heavy musings, which are faster than a Cray mainframe. "The mind is a terrible thing to waste" or better "To waste a mind is a terrible thing to do" or "The waste of the mind is the worst waste" make me hope that the act of thinking is at least a calorie-burning activity and/or a way to empty the memory banks so that there's room for more.

Jack's nine years of adventures could fill up a few memory banks themselves. He went camping in Alaska. He went to Majorca on an archaeological dig. He went hiking in the Pyrenees. He spent 25 days trekking the mountains in Nepal and surviving, barely, on yak cheese, the Sherpa's gruel, and Snickers. That trip began on the very morning that the "shoot to kill" curfew had been lifted in Nepal. Our papers did not report much about the king and the problems of Nepal; they also ignored the plight of Tibet when it was overrun and ransacked by the Chinese. In politics as well as in real estate the watchword is location, location, location.

Jack also went wilderness canoeing in Canada where he assisted in locating and labeling virgin pines. He's done the same for ferns in New Hampshire. Combining learning with adventure suits him since his love of reading, his energy, his friendliness and loyalty, all work together and urge him on.

Each time he went on one of those trips, he was out of communication. "On the dark side of the moon," Helen says, and she had the normal mixed emotions of trepidation and elation. But she also admired the ease and confidence with which Jack traveled the world. Helen's first plane ride was in a DC-3, and she had been forewarned not to panic if some flames spit out of the engines. Such an archaic plane is as difficult for today's kids to comprehend as being a teenager without a McDonald's. Her trip brought her all the way across Lake Michigan—a long way from home and from her generation. It was years later (when we stopped at my old Air Force base in Dayton and toured the museum) that she finally accepted the fact that the DC-3 was probably the safest plane ever built. Traveling by plane came full tilt after WWII, being accepted in only half a generation's time. Most of our friends have been to far-flung countries, countries our parents only read about in *National Geographic.* But still, Jack managed to raise traveling from the mundane to the adventuresome with his duffel bag and his trekking. He would never, as Thoreau warned, be surprised in old age to find out that he never had truly lived.

During those nine years, Jack used his vacations to escape from the daily suit-and-tie work and we enjoyed his trips vicariously. Meanwhile, Elizabeth and Brad presented us with three more grandchildren and the happy by-products of months of anticipation. Four boys would have been wonderful; four girls would have been wonderful; but two boys and two girls is beyond wonderful and into wondrous.

It was after Jack's trip to Majorca and Elizabeth's second baby that Hannah finally persuaded Helen and me to come to Hawaii, and to meet John. The timing was right. Helen was getting fidgety.

Helen: "Set the alarm for 7 tomorrow."
"What's tomorrow?"
Helen: "Tennis starts."

That Helen enjoys playing tennis is a fortuitous result of a risk the kids and I took when she turned 40. Tennis fervor had hit the land. Communities were building courts as if the overbuilding of bowling lanes in the 1970s had never been heard of. Everyone was urged to play. Good exercise and, what's more, indoor courts would make playing available year 'round, unlike golf. High schools and junior high schools built courts and had competitive teams. And Helen's friends again took up the game that they had dropped when they had married. But Helen had never played tennis: "I don't ice skate because my ankles are weak and I don't play tennis because my wrists are weak. So don't give me a racquet for my birthday! I don't know how and I don't want to know how to play tennis. I'm 40. Just because everyone else is doesn't mean I have to." The kids and I gave her a wooden, Chris Evert racquet.

Helen liked the game enough to give the kids racquets for their birthdays. She and Jack painted a court on the cul-de-sac in front of our house. They used green paint left over from Elizabeth's cleaning and painting of the basement. (I had paid her for the job when she couldn't find work one summer.) Having no net didn't bother them, but our neighbor who had been a champion player in college couldn't stand to watch their improper form. He came out and showed Helen how to serve: "Just like pitching a baseball." Her serve has been unorthodox ever since.

Then her friend and ex-roommate joined the new Tennis Center. "I was really nervous," Corinne said, "because I thought they'd all be hot-shots and wear fancy outfits and you know, the Country Club kind, but it's fun and we could play all winter." So Helen joined. She's played two and sometimes three times a week for 20 years, all because she had insisted we not give her a tennis racquet for her birthday.

These days, though, Helen needs 90 minutes to prepare: three cups of coffee, a few cigarettes, and a piece of toast just to wake up enough to read the newspaper. Then come the stretching exercises, clothing choices, and revving up to hit the ball decently. A couple of alley shots can make her morning. Last summer she gave up singles. Last Christmas Jack agreed to play rules for singles while she used doubles. Her edge of experience hadn't helped for years, and she says next time he'll have to play lefty. But tennis is her tomboy outlet. I benefit from her tennis too, because she can identify with the Pistons, Lions, Tigers, and understand the intensity and the thrill of a good play. She says football, especially in slow motion, looks like ballet. And, too, her solos on the sax have given her an empathy with all performers. "There are a jillion excellent musicians," she says, "but only thousands of people who don't get glue-mouth and slippery fingers and shortness of breath when 'Solo' is written on the upper left of a sheet of music." So we both anticipate and enjoy each season's sports, but I don't agree with her that banning the coaches and advisors from the Press Box would make better football games.

Given all that, there are more times lately when she returns from tennis and reports things like "I saw Jan today. She must be over 70. Nobody on that court *runs*."

And I say, "But she's out there. She's not sitting around eating chocolate pretzels." To which Helen replies with some of her rare but exquisite expletives. And, mentally, I second them.

We had glided through the middle-age crisis without noticing it, but now the *old* generation is *ours*, even though we're supposed to be ten years younger, physically, than the previous generation was at our age. And, since we are expected to live longer than they did, we are a real dilemma for the young,

Mirror, Mirror

The wicked witch cackles at me:
"Not the fairest. Not even fair."
What fun-house trick has warped the glass,
distorted my real image? My hair

once (yesterday?) curled
brunette upon my brow
framing smooth, high bones
in symmetry and grace … but NOW

I see a face with crinkled tracks
drawn down from squinty eyes and lips,
down from chins and cheeks.
No vanity uplifts

this mockery of fair maiden.
Who would praise such fallen charms!
Who but my gray-haired prince.
He will come. And take me in his arms.

Grandmother's Mementos

Words
in my wicker basket:
    "love, husband, children,
    worry, busy, happy, proud,
    nice young lady, fine
    young man, write often,
    love, farewell,"
Words,
worn smooth by memory's caress,
buried near my rocking chair
under tangled skeins of years.

productive element, those still paying into Social Security while we, at the other end, are taking money out. Whatever conclusion comes from this debate, we have the deep awareness that *we are next!* That awareness gave us the extra little push we needed to go to Hawaii and see Hannah—that, plus remembering that Nick had girded his loins and taken a wild airplane ride through snowstorms just to give Helen a hug when their mother was dying, so Helen had to give Hannah a hug even if the emergency was a bit cooled off and might be only sirening in Helen's mind.

Once we made the decision to go, Helen took her usual pugilist stance against Fate. On the plane she covered her face by reading a book by Sheldon, which distracted her from mentally having to raise the flaps of the plane and/or guide it through turbulence. During the long flight, we both tried not to remember the "real, imitation turkey feathers," the jolly times, all those years.

We met Hannah and John at their favorite outdoor lunch spot. We sat next to a waterfall in a lavish garden with tons of maile that gave off the most perfumy airs. And we got another chance to prove that man and melons are hard to know. Nothing about John reminded us of Jube. He was shorter than Hannah. His humor was sober. His hands were worker's—not dirty but stubby-fingered and rough, chewed up with cuts and scrapes. He was slender, agile, tanned, and he did not talk with his mouth full.

Helen asked, "Have you lived in Diamond Head a long time?"

John: [chew, chew, chew, chew, swallow] "About ten years."

"And all that time you made baskets?"

John: [chew, chew, chew, swallow] "No, all that time I repaired houses."

Hannah volunteered, "He's fixed dozens of houses. You'd think they'd just been built!"

Hannah smiled at John. Helen smiled at me. I smiled, so help me, at John. He took another forkful of pasta and added a prong of celery. I waited. Then I quickly jumped in, "Where did you learn your trade?"

But he waited until he picked up a forkful of pasta, and chewed, and swallowed, and then replied, "I learned it by doing it."

So I couldn't resist: "In that case, may we see your first house?"

A tiny smile showed at the corner of the napkin as he wiped his mouth and Helen and Hannah laughed loudly. Thank goodness.

After 45 minutes of shouting innocuous comments over the splash of the water tumbling down the boulders, Hannah escorted us through her quiet little house, and it was obvious that she had found a kindred spirit in John. He had a touch for decorating. He hung pictures four or so feet from the floor or a few inches above a table. He explained that "eye-level is for art that is so bad it won't be noticed." He put bronze turtles under the end table. We exclaimed over each piece and each unusual fabric. Then we all stepped into the jungle of the small garden, walking a curvy path of colored figure-eight pavers, which I was praising when Helen did a dead stop in front of me.

"There's Woody!" she exclaimed, staring at a statue she had spotted under a hanging fig. "I mean, there's Woody's sister!" she added. Sure enough, we walked over to get a closer look. "Oh, how sweet she pulls her skirt aside and looks demurely downward as if contemplating a mud puddle," said Helen, always imaginative. "She and Woody should be side by side. What's her name?"

John looked blank. Hannah repeated "Name?"

Helen said, "Surely she has one?"

Hannah said, "Well, no. I never thought about a name. She was here when I came."

So Helen volunteered, "Wanda?"

John, looking back and forth from me to Helen, asked, "Who

is Woody?"

Helen said, "Why, didn't Hannah tell you? She and Jube surprised us with a statue for our garden. We named him Woody and he's the same height and style as Wanda except he's a boy."

Helen looked at Hannah. "I can't believe you didn't tell him," she said.

Hannah said she never thought of boring John with such silliness, that Helen's imagination was a bit strong sometimes, that for all she knew Jube had put this Wanda-girl out there because the previous owners were friends of his, that Jube got strange ideas sometimes, and that we should all go in for some tea and she had some pineapple for it. "Pineapple?" whispered Helen, after recovering from Hannah's quick explanation. Hannah jabbers that John likes a chunk of pineapple in his iced tea, and we should all try it, and we say, "when in Rome … ."

We sat in the pleasant sunroom that was absolutely full of plants of all colors, sizes, and shapes either hanging or sitting or even lying down, and there we had little sandwiches. I wanted to fish out the pineapple from my tea and ask for a lemon slice, but I didn't because I was watching John shake his sandwich. The bread triangle between his thumb and two fingers was not dripping mayo but his wrist went up and down, up and down, like a gentle salt shaker. I watched for whatever might fall out and wondered if I was supposed to shake mine. Etiquette whispered, "Watch the hostess." So I turned my smiling gaze to Hannah who wasn't shaking her sandwich, and I looked at Helen who wasn't shaking her sandwich. Then I looked back at John who, I was happy to see, was merely chewing what he had been shaking. I thought all that chewing and shaking must drive Hannah crazy, but she chatted at my smiley gaze with the assurance that we'd been impressed with her set-up and will therefore stop being concerned about her.

All in all, the visit came off nicely, nicer than our reaction to Oahu and the throngs of people. Helen said, "Do you realize that not one waiter said 'There ya go'? What a relief!" It was true. On the mainland, we always play a dining-out game: For every "There ya go" we mentally cut 10% off the tip and figure how much the waitress or waiter would owe us if we presented the bill. I actually tip very generously. (Our daughter used to be a waitress when she was in high school.) Nevertheless, we flinch over the umpteenth "There ya go" from the bringing of coffee to the placement of the bill in the middle of the table. And if the cashier at the hotel returns my worn-down credit card with a "There ya go" instead of a 'Thank you very much! Please come again" or any reasonable facsimile, Helen fumes to me, "What's the matter with a simple 'Thank you'!" It is the manager, of course, who should be training his employees. I shudder to think what Helen will say when she is inflicted by the latest fad in bad customer relations as reported by Judy: "You guys want water? I'll bring you guys your change, okay? You guys need anything else?" Not a "thank you" in the room except when a customer accidentally says it after receiving the bill. But in Hawaii, the waiters were courteous, and as pleasant as the flowers.

Helen liked all the colors of flowers that were almost, not quite but almost, too blatant. I was impressed with the variety of orchids. Our northern flowers just seem to be more subdued. Of course, they have a tougher life and have to regrow each year or, as annuals, just give it up. The pina coladas were refreshing and everywhere was color, color, color and people, people, people. "But," Helen reflected, "it was claustrophobic what with the volcanoes and being surrounded by water. And it seemed fake, as if Disney had set it all up." Sounded like I could cross generic "Hawaii" off my list and move Scandinavian countries up a notch.

We evaluated John and decided he was a good companion for Hannah, who surely must have felt like a widow the past year. But still, John didn't give Hannah time—or, she didn't want it—

to have a heart-to-heart with Helen, which Helen chewed over and over all the flight home: "After all this time, you'd think she'd want to talk to me and tell me how she really feels."

I couldn't get by with "mnmph," so I said, "You two sisters are really kind of old to be giggling over boyfriends," and, of course, I immediately knew that was the wrong thing to say. It was too late to add my all-wise "mnmph," but Helen was too upset over Hannah to spare any upsettedness over me. I said that sometimes when people are truly hurting or truly happy, it's too great a thing to talk about; you have to give them time to let the edges rub off. And I added some examples and stuff and finally looked over my shoulder and saw that Helen had, as usual in the middle of my fine stories, dozed off. She never had dozed off on a plane before. I hoped distance and our own lively routine would let the Hannah-John thing settle down.

By Christmas Hannah wrote her usual bubbly letter, and Helen sent a bubblier one back, I'm sure. She said that whenever she tried to picture Hannah's house she saw instead "foam on the beach." So then she'd concentrate on the vision of Wanda but didn't write about Wanda or Woody in the letter because Hannah's remarks in her garden had had the effect of a sisterly warning, like, "Don't even think about borrowing my blue sweater." I admit to thinking about Wanda myself. It was obvious that Wanda and Woody were bought and delivered at about the same time, the vines and weeds being quite mature and the statues looking quite settled in, and indeed, looking like fraternal twins. Either Jube had taken a secret side trip to Hawaii that autumn of "the coming of Woody" when he had gone "to Canada to check on the amethyst," or serendipity and coincidence had a remarkable collision.

A business card came with Hannah's birthday note to Helen at the end of February: "Hanjohn's." It even sounded Hawaiian. We knew right away that the fine print would say, "Your inside/outside home decor center." What the fine print would not say was whether Hannah and John were centered together or separately. That part of their business was none of our business, of course. Helen remarked that Hannah certainly had a marvelous source somewhere for home decorating pieces, and I remarked that that seemed only natural since she ran an import business for years and would certainly still have connections.

Actually, I had thought that those turtles under the table had a strange gargoyle look to them, and I wouldn't have considered them marvelous pieces without Hannah's pointing out to me that they were. John's baskets were "marvelous" too—great spirally things that could never be used as baskets but would be great as "pieces." Obviously there are many, many people who like to have non-utilitarian objects sitting around their houses. Our house is mostly in an ongoing decorative stage: Helen "hangs and puts" instead of "places" and the "pieces" are her own creations which she changes with the seasons or whenever the mood strikes. But Hanjohn's wouldn't be selling to us. They would no doubt do a fine, brisk business with natives and tourists alike, since having a home on the islands is not a prerequisite for purchasing their objects of art. Gargoyle turtles can be under an end table in Minnesota just as seashells can be on a dresser in Arizona.

It was easier to put the Hannah-John thing on a back burner than I had thought it would be. For spring came again, and between the house and The Land we had plenty of chores to keep both of us busy. Just getting storms off and screens on took several weeks of reminders. Helen went rummaging for our spring/summer clothes, relegating the winter stuff to its months of hibernation in the basement dresser and the spare closets. Where did we put our out-of-season clothes before the kids' closets became available to us? And what do people in California do without the great climatic changes that necessitate shovels for snow, chemicals for ice, heating to bring minus 20 up to plus 65, and bird seed for starving birds, rabbits, and squirrels? We need rakes, fertilizers, weed-killers, long johns, boots, woolens of several densities, as well as shorts and short-sleeved shirts, sandals, and visors. The list that each new season requires is very long. What do Californians do with that extra time and money? Do they think up new wild hair styles, body piercings, and dances, not to mention other things that I certainly cannot imagine?

Anyway, we here in the northern Midwest understand Eliot's "April is the cruelest month." Not only do we have extra chores, but we usually put them into high gear on a balmy 60 degree day, only to be followed by "lows of 26" and the realization that spring is not actually here yet, it is only taunting us.

We are always anxious about the berry plants in April. Did they survive this harsh winter? How many blank spaces will there be? Did I measure the dormant weed killer right? Why aren't they at least showing signs by now? And then finally the day comes in May when we can see from the road that the ground has a green cast, and we know we'll soon be walking the rows finding errant weeds while the farmer's winter wheat—he alternates corn with soybeans with wheat—surrounds the berries with what looks like a big, lush, lawn of healthy, tall grass.

Each year I encroach on some more footage for berries or gardens. This spring, George will plant his garden. As the new retiree, George returns to tend to his roots, so to speak. Last fall I staked off a bit more than the year before. Our farmer watches out for these white stakes and plows up to them. He knows he has a good deal—the rent has been the same for 20 years—and he

Daily Bread

Who lifts the weary sun each day
and hurls it flashing on its way,
lift me!
Who guides its path with sure, high aim
past pointed stars too far to name,
guide me!

What holds up a newborn calf
on legs so wobbly we have to laugh,
hold me!
What tells the wren to sing and sing
as if her song were everything,
tell me!

Who helps the rose through winter's cold
while it is withered, dry, old,
help me!
Who shows it then when spring is here
that Life and Love were always near,
show me!

Powered by their primal source,
all things receive their proper course.
Even me?

usually tends to this little 12-plus acreage after he has finished with his other 450 acres. As long as he still has room to turn his big monster around, he'll not mind the nibbling I do on my own property.

This unusually cold April was hard to take. The tomato, squash, gourds, and melon seeds we had started indoors were already two inches tall, and we'd have to stall them until all danger of frost had passed, which is a real guessing-game. The bluebird houses sat there, waiting. Helen had covered the new magnolia bush about six times, each time thinking it would be the last time she'd have to haul out the yards of burlap and the two poles. The lilac buds sat there. The forsythia had a pathetic showing. All the seed packets had to wait until we could declare the ground warm enough. We were bored.

I had chopped enough firewood for two winters. Helen had chopped a path through the woods in preparation for better viewing of the trilliums. We even went to a movie. We rented a few VCR tapes, carefully selecting what was called humorous. (Richard Dreyfuss was generally a safe bet.) We sat through the three-minute trailers and credits wondering what sort of contract required listing the "third gaffer, second gaffer, first gaffer, caterer" et. al. and then running the names at a speed that defied anyone to read them. We decided it must be for the inside knowledge of the industry, not for the viewer's appreciation, and therefore they expected everyone in theaters or in their living rooms to get up and leave before the credits were finished. Another week of this dreary, cold weather and we'd probably have started to criticize PBS! Luckily the break came.

We drove out to The Land on a day of blue sky and balmy 58 degrees. Would the buds on the peach be unharmed? Are those flower buds or leaf buds again on the chestnut? Do you see any sign of the berries over there by the woods? I went over to check on the rototiller while Helen strolled toward the woods, and I heard her holler, "Woody's gone!" I looked up and sure enough, his head wasn't showing above last fall's dead weeds. We hurried over, confused by the fact that our eyes did not see him yet. We knew he couldn't go anywhere and that no one in all these years had thought he'd be worth the trouble to steal. Then we saw that he wasn't gone, just toppled over. We stared at him as if willing him to get up. I saw a gash on his back.

"He's been hit by something that doesn't look like a rifle shot," I said.

"They'd need your permission to hunt, wouldn't they?"

"Well, one year I gave it," I said, "but not this year."

"Well what then?"

"Let's try to set him up. You stand on the base and pull his head and I'll push."

Helen didn't move.

"How can I stand on the base when it's at a perpendicular?" she asked.

"Just stand on the top," I suggested.

"HOW CAN I STAND ON THE TOP WHEN IT'S ON ITS SIDE!"

"Helly, don't get excited. Just stand on that."

I put my hand on the rim or the side or the top or whatever it was technically called, and Helen sighed and stood on it. I pushed. He came right up.

Helen picked up a small piece of something that she thought had fallen off of him. She showed it to me. It was smooth and oblong and about two inches long.

"Oh, I hope it's not his nose. No, he's all there," she stammered. "So …"

"He's hit right between his shoulder blades. Must be at least six inches long. Whatever hit him really turned him around with some force."

"And here's a piece I can get out, Helen said. "And there's a little pile on the ground. What are those? They look like stones but here's a squarish one, and a roundish one, and here's an oblongish one. They fell out of him!"

"Reminds me of those abbey ruins we saw in Oxford," I said.

"You're right! They filled the walls with rubble!"

"It made such beautiful sense, and I never guessed it."

Helen asked, "You think Woody's full of this?"

"Looks like it."

"Then let's tip him over again," Helen suggested.

"No," I said, "Let's just lean him over. I'll get cement blocks from the barn."

We leaned Woody backward against the square end of the weighted wheel barrow, and a few more stones fell out. Then I put the blocks on the ground. We leaned him against them, and more fell out. Helen gathered them up in a pail and asked if we should empty him entirely. We'd have had to make the gash bigger to do that, so we quit our efforts, righted Woody, and took the rubble home to wash it off. It looked like gray/black washed stones in various sizes and shapes.

Helen said, "All this time I thought he was solid."

"So did I. It wouldn't do any good to empty his ballast. We'd just have to fill him up with something else."

"That turned out to be a lot less exciting than I thought it would be, finding him, and then finding him gashed, and then finding him just filled with rubble. You'll have to patch him up."

"Why don't you? I've got enough stuff to do here now, or those weeds will be our only garden this year."

"What with?"

I said, "Probably your craft store has something. Unless you want to affix a mesh and apply fresh concrete, and wait till it dries, and then …"

"Never mind. I'll find something, but it won't be easy explaining what I want it for."

That night our farmer phoned and apologized for "nicking

our statue," explaining that he didn't actually do it himself but had sent out a hand to deepen that drainage that runs through the wheat. He told me he turned the tractor around, and even though it was his smallest tractor, its blade hit something that sounded like a boulder but turned out to be the statue. He would gladly pay for it, and he was very sorry. I replied that it was okay. We could fix it. Accidents happen. We left it the way we left other accidents such as the lopping off of a Norway spruce. Accidents happen when people live together on the same planet, so we allow for that. Besides, Lord knows I've done my share of dumb things and will probably do more any day. Helen quoted my oft-stated philosophy, "It's the unpredictableness of farming that keeps it from being dull." She made a wry face but accepted the rather dull explanation for what we had halfway hoped was a very unusual happening. This time I was the one who thought the whole thing was weird, including the rubble. But Helen put the stones in a box in the basement and said that someday she'd probably use them for something.

Cool April was followed by cool May and sunless June. On July 1 we took off for Yellowstone, happy to see sunshine and to get across the flooded Midwest without problems. Helen, cowering in the trailer, survived two storms. We returned to Michigan via the glorious open roads of the unpopulated northern route over Lake Superior, and before going to see if our house was still standing, we stopped at The Land to see if the barn was still standing and the crops still growing despite our six weeks' absence.

The property looked the same as when we had left, but the garden was buried in lush weeds and the tomatoes that we managed to find were still quite green. The raspberry bushes were very tall and had many tiny flowers. "A second banner season," flitted across our souls. By September the tomatoes were still green, the squash small, the corn spindly, and the berries slow to ripen. Tons of them sat there in their pale pink intimation of the red to come.

Pickers came on schedule, but they had to walk an entire 325' row to get their two or three quarts. Where there should be dozens of ripe berries there were, here and there, a few. People said it had been a cool, sunless July while we had been enjoying the warmth of the west, but we assured them that probably next week would be the peak of the season. Next week turned into the next and the next. We felt like liars even though the sympathetic people agreed that it was the weather's fault, and they had their own green tomatoes to prove it. The unpredictableness of farming was getting to be more annoying than fun. I thought we ought to close early, but Helen thought we ought to warn our loyal customers. The next day we started telling everyone that things looked iffy so would they please call our number for a taped message before coming out to the patch.

On the final Saturday morning of our miserable season, about 20 minutes before closing, an old Ford clattered up the long driveway. We tried to figure out who it was and wondered how to break the news to a new customer that we were closing for the season. We stood next to the table of quart boxes at the parking lot edge while the Ford pulled into the space between our Buick and pickup even though the entire lot was otherwise empty. A stocky man hopped out and smiled at me as I walked over. I racked my brains. Who *is* he? Am I supposed to remember him? From work? Someone Helen knows? I started to apologize for the crop and the weather and our very existence out here; but he interrupted to say he'd heard about our place, and he declared it to be a nice spread. And then he simply asked, "Seen Jube lately?"

Bombshell! My kneecaps started to slip.

Splutter mode kicked in: "J-Jube?" Helen stayed put at the table, gathering the boxes and pails and belts.

"Yeah. Jube. Guess I oughta introduce myself. Name's Pack. Knew Jube way back. Told me how he'd come here, Mr. Hilarious, and so I was on my way to the C & O docks and … ."

He continued to explain, but only one word caught me and echoed like the loudest goose call in an overhead honking: "Hilarious." Jube had heard my name-story enough to have fallen asleep over it. *Who is this guy?* I resorted to another splutter: "Jube?"

"Hey," he said, "if you don't want the wife to know … ."

I asked, calmly, "What did you say your name is?"

He said, "Pack. Call me Pack. Only the IRS calls me by longer names. As I said, if the wife … ."

He put out both hands, palms up as if to ward off a spray from some jokester with a hose, a lighthearted gesture, as if we were conspirators in a negotiation—but I didn't know what the hell we were negotiating. It flashed into my head that maybe he was fishing, too.

"Sorry," I said, "I don't know any Jube. We sell raspberries here and are about to close for the season, so if you'll come back next September … ." My brain hurt from trying to think fast while desperately hoping he didn't see the flicker of interest in my eyes. I told myself that eyeball-watching is a fiction spread by cowboy gunslingers and football quarterbacks. Pack was talking again, about going somewhere and having a beer, and "settling this."

I hoped I had nothing to lose by stonewalling. I walked to his other side so I could see Helen and casually held up my hand on its way to adjust my cap. She raised her hand and started folding the table. We had that hand signal stuff for whenever we met someone we knew very well but couldn't remember the person's name and didn't want to be caught in an embarrassing introduction. I was relieved to see her smiling assumption that we'd go over the alphabet later, trying to stir up a clue to the right name.

Then I said, "Mr. Pack, I'd like to help you out with this Jube person, but since I don't know what you're talking about, I'm afraid you'll have to search somewhere else. Have you called the police?" As soon as I heard that leaving my mouth I knew it was a mistake: he never implied Jube was missing! But he ignored me and began to talk with a tinge of nostalgia, like someone who's had a few too many beers, about good ol' Jube and their good times together when they met at the dock and how he was the main man for the import stuff.

I perked up. "At Ludington?" I nudged, hoping I might get some idea about Jube myself.

"Naw," he said, "Milwaukee."

He moved closer and put his heavy paw on my shoulder. I felt myself slipping again into another slip of the tongue, and although I thought Pack not too bright, I couldn't get reckless. I didn't even know the man. Helen drove past in the Buick, yelled her usual "see you later" and headed home. Pack removed his paw from my shoulder, rested it on my jacket lapel and said, ominously, "I really need to talk to Jube. He owes me. I did a lot for him."

My mind registered scenes of gangsters making offers people couldn't refuse. A black car turned up the drive. "This isn't happening!" I muttered. Pack removed his paw and stepped back and gave his shoulders a henchman's shrug and then I realized it was Bill in the black car, his Taurus that he loved. He cheerfully called out, "Hope I'm not too late!" Bill was an old friend and regular customer! I almost ran over to him. When he explained that his wife needed a quart for her dessert for book club, I immediately offered to help him pick. "No berries" never means "absolutely none at all."

We started out to the rows with Pack clomping his heavy steps. He said "Name"s Pack" and Bill said "Bill" and they shook hands. "Say, Bill, you being a good friend to Hilarious here, maybe you know Jube?"

Bill laughed his deep chuckle, stopped at an underripe bunch of berries, picked up the cane to check for hidden gems and answered, "Mr. Hilarious! You got that right. Hank here's the funniest fellow I've ever known."

Pack persisted, "So do you know Jube?"

I realized this was heading towards Bill's total confusion and perhaps my loss of some teeth, so I said, "Pack, why don't we meet at the barn after I help this *paying customer*." After a glare, he stomped off.

Bill chuckled some more. "Did he want free berries?" he asked.

I said, "No, just keep picking and listen to me. That guy is a stranger, and I can't get rid of him. Don't ask questions. Just leave normally and ask Norm to come out in an unmarked car, no sirens."

Bill paused, looked at me, and said, "You got it" just as if we were roommates untangling a blind date snafu again. I hoped his old heart was as strong as our friendship. Mine was beating too darn hard, but I blew my nose and took a deep breath as Bill ambled off yelling, "See you next September." To Pack he said, "Last chance to get the best berries in town." Off he went, without spinning the tires. And now it's my turn, I thought, to act cool.

I walked slowly toward the barn, tried to get a handle on my options: How long can I stall, waiting for Norm? Or should I tell Pack that I know Jube, that I don't know where he is, that I'm worried about him, that Pack could help me by explaining a few things about his friendship with Jube? But he doesn't know where Jube is either, so what good would it do? He's strange in a dumb sort of way but probably not dangerous but he did sort of threaten me and looks like he would need only one punch to knock me out except that would be really dumb, quieting the guy who supposedly had the answer but he's trespassing but my God, we are open to the public! Pack accompanied me to the truck where I casually put my foot on the back bumper and calmly removed a boot.

"Now, start over," I said in my best we're-going-to-settle-this tone.

Pack set his thick legs firmly apart, stuck his hands in his jacket pockets—a pose that gesture analysts would call "dominating"—and said, simply, "Me and Jube had a deal going, but I ain't mad. I just think he forgot. So I thought why not look him up, and he'd probably be glad to see me. Like I said, we go way back and I gotta catch the 3:30. But Jube would really 'preciate seeing me."

I thought, If he thinks Jube would be glad to see someone he owes money or whatever to, he doesn't know him well at all, but I said, "If I could help you, I would. I can't. So now you are really trespassing so why don't you leave. And good luck." I don't know why I added that. Maybe I meant it for me. Thank goodness I didn't add, "Let me know if you find him," which was on the way out of my mouth when I threw the boots in the front seat, got in, and started backing. What if he feels too frustrated, lets me leave and then, then sets the barn on fire?

Pack ambled alongside the truck, put his face into the open window and very quietly said, "It's amber. Amber. I got it for him!"

I stopped. I saw Jube and Hannah and pieces of amber floating in the sky above Pack's head, and I heard my high laugh and my repeating, "Amber? Amber? Pipe stems?" I drove to the gate with Pack's hand on the door handle as he pounded alongside. And the prayed-for unmarked car came up.

"How you doing, Hank?" asked Norm, all gussied up with his badge and pistol.

Pack looked thunderstruck. I guess intimidation made him blurt out without even being asked, "Mr. Hilarious here and me was just talking."

Norm looked around. "Where's this Mr. Hilarious?" he asked.

Pack stammered, "Hank, er, here, er."

Norm being all business turned to me and asked, "Mr. Virtson, do you want this man to leave?"

I looked at Pack and in my best boldness said, "I guess it was all a case of mistaken identity."

Relieved, Pack said, "You're really not Mr. Hilarious?"

And I, all strong now, said, "No. I'm not."

I unlocked the gate. Pack grumbled, "Hell. Much obliged for nothing, Jube. A fake name yet! Shoulda seen it coming the way he acted last time and then not showing up. Hell." He walked back to his car, and then, as if to make sure no trouble would follow him, he said a brusque, "Sorry, just a mistake" to Norm, and drove past us and, hopefully, out of our lives.

I thanked Norm for interceding in a possibly explosive situation and poured out my admiration for policemen who know what to do in every sticky situation. Norm was visibly pleased and acknowledged that he was just doing his job and that some days it's easier than others. Since no charges were brought we'd all forget the whole thing. I thought "fat chance" but smiled at him, again gave him my deepest thanks, and stared after him as he sped off to answer a fender-bender on Wheeler and Jefferson.

Bill's car came up. He leaned out the window, and I gave him my deepest thanks too, which was all I seemed to be able to do while relief robbed my head of any sensible reaction except gratitude. Bill predictably said, "No problem," and added, "Want to tell me about it?" I said that as soon as I figured it out, I would, and meanwhile would he please not mention the little incident to Helen or anyone? He answered,"You got it," and drove off. They don't make friends like that anymore.

At least Helen wouldn't be wondering why I was so late, since I've often been stuck with a new customer who would have just been driving by and would have seen our U-PICK sign. We wouldn't have to go through the alphabet after all.

I found myself not going straight home, but driving north across Wheeler until I was next to the most recent oil rig of the many that suddenly appeared around our Land during the oil crunch. This one was working—like those toy chickens that bob up and down for water, only it was black and looked more like the neck and head of an unusual breed of horse. I watched it go slowly up and down, unattended but doing its job all day and all night, mesmerizing.

I thought about Pack. What exactly had he said about the docks? Meeting Jube? Think. Think. Forget those goofy ideas about burning barns and mafia and think about gruffy Pack meeting Jube at those deserted C & O docks. We've taken those ships lots of times, the old City of Midland … two kids along and not even a candy bar for sale … unloading at inconvenient hours, like 3 a.m. When would they have chosen to meet? The way Pack acted, probably after the 3 a.m., the one least likely to have many passenger cars with the trains. And Pack had said amber.

This was no coincidence. Ships … the Navy! Oh man, I can see it now. That old Tiz-It tavern at the entrance to the dock-yards. Jube would be standing, waiting, in front of the flickering, neon "Closed" sign while the noisy, two-hour unloading of the railroad cars dragged on. I can picture it just as sure as if I were a mouse, or rather, a well-fed rat watching from behind the over-flowing trash barrel:

"That old hunk o' steel come sideways again?"

"Godamighty, we got hung up at Toronto. Too damn many chiefs over there. Then the sou'easter switched north on us. That leaky laker ain't long for this world! She's the oldest old crone, gettin' uglier by the second. Geez, I'm gettin' too old for this."

"Yeah, yeah, Hand it over."

"Three little ones this time."

"Good. When's your next call?"

"Dunno."

"What do your mean?"

"Like I said, I'm gettin' too old for this. This ain't the Navy y'know. I wuz thinkin' the last time, I oughta get on that new baby. She's 1,000. Too big for the Seaway hassle. Just cruises from Minnesota to Indiana. Now that would be just a piece o' cake."

"What about my stuff?"

"I could find ya someone. Most think the ocean's easier anyway. Hell, these cantankerous lakes—kick up in the middle just when I'm settled in. Now those stiff jobs take the ocean easy as pie. Must be 50 to 100 here from Bombay, Russia, you name it."

"One more. Just one more. I'll set it up. Three months from now."

"We ain't got no breaker, y'know. Could be shut down by December 10 the way things are goin'. Sweetest words in the English language: Great Lakes' Shipping Ceases. The Lawrence will shut down and your stuff will be frozen till spring and I'll be sitting in this here bar laughing my head off. Ya can call me here."

"Hell, you know it won't work that way. Look, for this last one, I'll double your share."

"Ya sure it'd be one, just one?"

"Hey, one old salt to another."

"Well … Maybe a hot bath, and a few beers, and some time with Tillie … Well, okay. One more. But that's it, so you better make it good. I'm too old for that sneakin' around. Ya just come here and hold out yer hand. Ya oughta try meeting some slob ya never saw before in some joint ya dunno who's who."

"You scared, Pack?"

"Scared! This ain't the first time, ya know. How far back da ya wanna go? Back to the ship? Hell I'm scared. You should be, too, but yer too stupid to be scared. Once more. Once more and I'll be free o' ya."

"Free o' me? Whatcha gonna do about yer greed then, ol'

buddy?"

"And that's another thing. Don't imitate me anymore. So you talk better. You don't deliver the stuff and without me you'd be nothing."

"Okay, okay! Don't get riled up. I'll see you exactly three months from today at the same time and we'll settle up once and for all."

Then these two guys would step back from each other, turn and walk in opposite directions, and then suddenly swing off as if someone had pulled them like a string of taffy, slowly, until the break sent them looping down and away in a quick swing. Yup, as a well-fed rat used to the ways of the docks, I could have described it all and quite well, too. But even as a rat, I'd have no one to squeal to. But it sure fits. Jube must have spent many hours with Pack over the years, sharing family pictures, even going so far as to talk about me as "Hilarious" when he knew it was a joke … playing Pack for a fool … Wonder where Pack will look now? "He owes me," he said. I got a feeling Pack is going to look until he finds him. If he does, we still won't know anything! Enough. I'll have to just keep alert. Can't unload all this junk on Helen.

The more days that passed innocently by, the more I kept hearing "Three can keep a secret if two of them are dead," and "Liar, liar, pants on fire, nose as long as a telephone wire." Kid stuff come back to haunt. Finally Helen asked if it was time for a trip, or was I going to frown for the rest of our lives.

Neither of us felt like enduring a journey to a far-flung, exotic place, since our fourth grandchild was due in November and we needed to love him/her into our world. We opted for the familiar camping up north: total relaxation, a bit of late-season golf on unflagged courses, time to think. I thought, all right. I thought "Amber, amber, imports, Jube, Hannah, Pack, amber … ."

It was the fourth day of thinking, and I'd not figured out a thing about my private puzzle. Helen was reading *Smithsonian* magazine while I was dozing in the hammock.

H: You should read this. Are you awake?

"Hmmmphg"

H: Did you know the Germans and Russians are all looking for very valuable amber that disappeared during The War?

I said, calmly, "M-m-m. I'll read it later" and feigned sleepiness while my heart beat AMber ... AMber ... AMber ... amBER ... amBER.

The article gave me a new respect for amber. In true *Smithsonian* thoroughness, it traced its importance from the Stone Age carvings through the Roman's use of it as good luck on warriors' coats of mail, the 18th century's Amber Room, which was covered entirely with fitted, hand-carved pieces, to today's intrigue with its perfectly embedded insects that are millions of years old. I knew it could make my arm hair stand up. But I didn't know that it carried along in salt water (and could therefore be found on some beaches) or that it was a lot more colorful than epoxy when the sunlight exploded inside or when it was heated.

But I kept returning to the vision of that room that disappeared from a Baltic port when the Nazis spirited away boxes of amber just before the end of the war. Over 100,000 invaluable pieces that heads of state and soldiers and regular civilians were all interested in finding. They looked in salt mines and in old ice cellars, and chased after every lead—small pieces of various shapes and sizes that were priceless. The price of regular good amber was soaring by tens of thousands of dollars. Small pieces of various shapes—some like squares, some round, some, some ... The image of our box of stones rose slowly over the lines on the page.

Back home I took advantage of Helen's absence one evening to have another look at Woody's stones. I carefully placed them on my workbench. I remembered the article stated, "Amber has a specific gravity between 1.05 and 1.10, so it sails in salt water." I had to lick my lips several times and clean my glasses twice while I searched for the perfect plastic pail. I found one Helen used to bleach her white jeans. Okay. I filled it with tap water, poured in some Kosher pickling salt, dropped in another stone and stirred the water with my finger, and waited. The stone sank. I put in three more. They sank. I dumped in the rest. They lined the bottom. What a relief!

Helen came back from bridge club "high" from all the exciting girl-talk:

"You still up?" she said. "It's 11:30! How long did you nap?"

"Helly, I've got something to tell you." She sat down, and her face went so serious I had to add quickly that it was more funny than serious. She kicked off her shoes, went to get her 7-Up and Late Times nightcap, and sat down to listen, knowing that no matter how I eased into it, this would have to be serious, to her if not to me, because we never ever cautioned each other before delivering a talk, preferring to broach unpleasant subjects in the middle of some pleasant chore. A hundred catastrophes probably flitted through her mind: dear, we're more broke than I thought; dear, he's all right now, but; dear, I got a part-time job. No, she'd never think that! I plunged ahead and told her the whole story about Pack at The Land and Bill and Norm, then the article, and then my stone experiment. Her eyes got wider and wider. She didn't ask one question and didn't interrupt me once.

When I finished and sat there looking at her, waiting for either an explosion or incredulity or fear, she suddenly burst into hysterical fits of laughter! Between wiping her tears and blowing her nose, she choked out, "And *you* accuse *me* of having a wild imagination!" I certainly wasn't prepared for that and started to defend myself by saying how worried I was that the stones might actually *be* amber. She settled into loud sniffy snorts.

I defended myself again: Do you have any idea of how our lives would have been irrevocably changed if those stones actually had been parts of missing, invaluable amber? The abominable newsmen with their "How does it feel?" and "What will you do with the money?" and all the trampling around our yard and lack of privacy and offers for made-for-TV movie and, what am I thinking! It would be a court case and an investigation and years of haranguing and harassing … .

"Maybe, though, it would have flushed Jube out from wherever he is if he is anywhere," Helen said.

"More likely he'd be hunted and have to go deeper into exile. It wasn't exactly a legal maneuver, you know."

"My gosh, Hank. We're talking as if we're thinking that the stones *are* amber."

"Well, that Woody-Wanda thing got me hoping it might somehow lead us to Jube. And there's that Pack guy."

Helen said, "I thought you said to let 'sleeping dogs lie.' Now you're acting like an amateur sleuth. Jube probably has twenty such people in his past the way he wheeled and dealed and Hannah never knew what was going on."

I added to my amateur image by saying, "That's another strange thing. She's so calm."

"We don't know that for sure. She might have cried her eyes out for months. And now she finally has some order in her life, and companionship, and dependability, and common interests."

"Helly," I said, "the stones sank. The whole thing is over. My torturous imaginings are finally over. I hated keeping them to myself, but I truly believed you'd be the one to flip out if I told you what I thought before I had any proof."

"Why would I flip? Who handled all the house and kid emergencies all those years? Who never ever phoned you at work except for that one time when Patch ran away?"

Helen came over and sat on my lap and teased, "I'm glad I can still surprise you, still keep you guessing."

Afterward, Helen again tried to stifle her giggles. I was somewhat peeved, and I threatened to get a hunk of cheese and turn on the light. She said, "No, it's not that. It's the amber! You really *are* Mr. Hilarious, you know." I listened to muffled giggs for what seemed like half an hour, and all the while I really wanted a chunk of Camembert, on a cracker.

The knitting needles click, click away the years of my memories. I look at Helen—so contented with our wonderful children, our superior grandchildren, our extraordinary and good marriage. I have riches indeed, more than I deserve. Because for the last two years I've been remembering a dream I had the night after the Pack confession. And I dreamed it again all this month.

I don't usually dream. Helen has said that everyone has dreams and if I don't remember any, that doesn't mean that I don't have any. But this dream was so vibrant that I remembered it all. If it had a message, I couldn't decipher it. If it didn't, why did it bother me? What would Helen make of it? Too much, surely. So, I didn't tell her.

For two years we just had our usual fun like camping up north in October, and one afternoon we went to see the Thunderbirds do their thing. We and hundreds of others waited on the East Bay beach. We picnicked, swam, and read. When 1:44 ticked by, we sat hushed in anticipation of the 1:45 arrival of the planes over the water. There was nothing. Then a roar from behind us lifted us to our feet with an ancient adrenaline rush, and five planes swooped low and veered straight up, circled, flew upside-down, and—well, anyone who has seen this display of impossible flying knows it can't be done, much less described.

After the show, we hurried to the airport, stood at the chain fence at the end of the runway and awaited the landing. Three planes roared in formation as if to land but at the last second, gunned it and zoomed off over our heads. We grabbed the fence. "Showoffs," Helen whispered at the planes, already distant silver points. We released the quivering fence and laughed short gasps of relief and amazement. Man, I was proud of those flyers!

Each season we found something that entertained or inspired us. And so the seasons passed, and then two years were gone. How can I now tell Helen that two years ago on that night of her hilarious hysteria, I dreamed a vivid, startling scene in which I saw the abbey in England being built, saw the rubble inside the walls, and was magnetically drawn to stare up at the cornice where these words were carved: **LOOK DEEP INTO THE PAST WHERE THE FUTURE LIES BURIED**. How can I ever begin to explain that I actually obeyed, sort of, that dream two whole years later—in fact, yesterday morning.

I was hauling firewood from the woods, struggling to push the wheelbarrow through the tall weeds past Woody, and I swore a bit at him and thought it would be nice if he'd do his fair share of work around here. I straightened out my aching back and studied the out-of-control grape vines circling and twisting all over his ever-youthful body and his beguiling smile. And right then, words seemed to jump from his mouth: **LOOK DEEP.** I stood there. Where had I heard those words? Had I read them somewhere? Did Helen quote one of her far-out philosophical tomes? I bent to pick up a couple small logs that had fallen off and saw a stone that looked familiar. Some sort of twilight zone happening here, I thought, as I realized the stone was not the Indian arrowhead that I wish I'd find just once. So why am I attracted to it? It's just a piece of rubble … The amber escapade! And then the dream came back. The chiseled words on the cornice with all the u's like v's.

I ran to the barn, got the iron bar, pried Woody over, ripped off Helen's patch job, and every stone that tumbled out from each repeated lurching of Woody I threw as if it were a hot rivet into the wheelbarrow. After sweating Woody upright again, I drove the three miles home without actually seeing the road, grabbed the pickling salt, drove back to The Land and added the salt to the stored water in the garbage pail in the barn and started dropping the stones one by one into the pail as I sloshed the water gently around. Ten stones sank mercifully to the bottom. The eleventh stone sank. I thought, "Helen's going to call me Mr. Hilarious again!" I dropped stone after stone and finally scooped up handfuls and dumped them in. They bubbled to the bottom except for some pieces of debris floating just under the surface. All the stones sank! I had done it again! Ridiculous to listen to a statue and a dream like they're messages from the gods.

I cut a hole in the bottom of the pail and let the water run out, and when I looked at the pile of stones I'd have to haul back to Woody, a golden gleam caught my eye. Four golden gleams sitting on top of the pile. I picked them out. Without breathing, I added water and salt to a berry pail and dropped the gleaming stones in and my shaking hands sloshed them just about right. They floated just below the surface like little boats up and down with the little waves. I stared at them and willed them to drown. They floated.

Like a robot—as if my mind were watching my body from some high vantage point and all its movements were in slow motion—I picked out the stones. Their unusually shaped curves fit each other like a puzzle, but I couldn't make out any actual design on their parts. Parts! Parts of the eagle maybe. After all, the entire room was missing—all 100,000 parts! I put them in my pocket and hauled the garbage pail full of rubble back to Woody. I scooped out handful after handful of the rubble and stuffed it back though the gash, and sweat ran into my eyes. Still I bent down and up, down and up, scoop after scoop sending twinges across my neck. Finally the garbage pail was empty. I reached into my pocket, took out the pretty amber pieces and dropped them through the gash. I replaced Helen's sticky repair slab over the hole, arranged all the vines around Woody's body and rubbed some dirt on his arms and face.

Last night we ate popcorn and watched the flames spit and snarl from the moist birch logs I had hauled home. Helen was blissfully unaware how my mind was lurching up and down with the flares, "Tell her! No, don't. Tell her now! No, don't." And it lurched that way most of the night, and now on this calm, pleasant morning the clicking, clicking of her needles seems like loud seconds ticking the countdown until I will eventually erupt and yell, "I've ruined our lives!"

I stand and tell Helen I'm going to get more wood, drier wood. She nods without looking up while her mouth forms the familiar movement of counting stitches.

I sit on the ground, wait for my breath to come back, look up at Woody and think, "What the hell am I going to do?"

Clouds move slowly over the meadow casting shadows that come towards me along the ground; freezing raindrops slip down Woody's cheeks and cling to the vines like rows of clear pearls. I think how pretty that would look on Wanda and how smart Helen was to never have written her sister about all our shenanigans. "How could I? she had asked. " How could I write that we suspected Jube all these years? It certainly wouldn't be funny to her!" No, it isn't funny. It's beating 20,000,000 to 1 odds and hating it.

But, nothing has actually changed! Three can keep this secret, because one of them is probably dead by now and one of them is a statue! "**THE FUTURE**" means someone else will discover "**THE PAST**" years and years from now, someone who will find a lilac bush and parts of a statue. Someone who will have spent his life researching and investigating will become famous and will deserve and welcome the fame! Maybe he'll use his archaic Desert Storm satellite receiver, or a newer model on his wrist that will tell him where amber is—just as archaic probably as Jack's old metal detector—but he won't be rich enough to get the latest thing. Adventurers never are rich. Of course, his wife could find Woody, all broken, and pick up an amber piece and put it on her kitchen windowsill next to the specially fine Petoskey stone. And when she's mechanically wiping the counter, her eye will catch the sunlight raying out from the millions of years of captivity, and, she'll be pleased.

The sun bursts out and sparkles Woody's face with a new twinkle in his eye and a new curve to his smile—that old contagious, all-knowing smile!

I flop back spread eagle and watch the old turkey buzzard do his high circling, circling. I wonder what he thinks, seeing this old guy lying on the ground with a giddy grin on his face.

PART II

Spring showed her intentions by popping up daffodils under the Burning Bush under Elizabeth's bedroom window, yellow brightly cheerful against our redwood ranch. By the time the midseason tulips sprout, the rabbits and in-city deer will have eaten their fill of daylily leaves, and the tulips might actually be permitted to flower.

"We're being overrun by deer and raccoons, Helly," I complained. "Better deer and raccoons than spiders and ants," said Helen.

At The Land, grapevines send their annual tendrils across Woody's face, but he still smiles. He knows their burying game would have its futile end in withering leaves by November, even though through summer they cover him until he looks like a Hollywood Roman instead of the Greek embodiment of beauty he thinks he exemplifies. Ah, yes, don't we all? We aren't that estranged from Woody's innocent delusion. Mirrors tell us lies from our right to our left; the truth about ourselves can never be known by us. But I am incapable of being demoralized. I am newly empowered by release from my Great Amber Ambivalence, and, I have got my boat 'n motor.

Good timing once again showed us ever-anxious mortals that there is a season for everything. Years ago a boat 'n motor would have been redundant, though I didn't know it then, what with three people eager to row our aluminum Bluegill—a name that belies our fishing for, but hardly ever catching, big bass and/or walleye and/or anything big. Then as time went by, Helen and I found it harder and then too hard to heave the boat up onto the car's roof, so I rigged up pulleys and hoisted the boat above our heads in the garage where it stayed, unused but not forgotten. But today, I already have the 1/2 ton truck/camper, so hauling the boat behind for three days in the woods along the Rifle River should be a snap. The guys are retired and ready anytime. We won't have to get in line to launch on busy weekends.

It was Helen who gave me the final push, insisting I use some of her inheritance that was idling in bonds. She decided that we should "spur our horses and gallop past our Puritan heritage of extreme caution before it's too late." Or something like that.

"We can afford a boat ourselves, you know," I said.

"I know. But it'd be fun to have it be free—like when Mom would buy me a book or a blouse when my weekly budget didn't quite make it," Helen insisted.

"Now you're going way-y-y back."

"Not so very far. When you built the addition for her …"

"It wasn't for her."

"… and we had only, what, $1200 left, total, including every nickel and we had no investments."

I said, "That's when I started the college fund."

"And it all worked out. And now I've got an idea how we can change the spare room into a sunroom and get a china cabinet so I don't have to stand on a chair to get the dishes from above the refrigerator. Then we could replace the aluminum sliding door, and—all sorts of improvements that we could have spent money on but didn't want to. Now we have this free money to blow. It's not like 'Funding of tonight's program was made possible with a grant from the Helen A. Virtson Foundation.' Gee, that must be something to have monies that go on and on for generations."

I said, "It'd be awful, all right. All those beggars bothering us day and night. Two hundred lawyers you'd have to trust. No thanks."

"Well, Hank, this is just monopoly money for us, so let's blow Marvin Gardens or Park Place. You surely don't think that what we don't do in our sixties we're going to do in our seventies!"

Seventies? Seventies? When my dad was seventy, when my mother was seventy—I must have been busy, because I only know that they once were seventy. I never knew or asked how they *felt* being seventy. How could Helen and I possibly be thinking of being seventy when I still feel like fifty, or even forty-five. But our kids are in their thirties! Was it so long ago that Helen told me, after the kids were in bed, "This afternoon Elizabeth and I were riding bikes down Ashman sidewalk, and she was in front and when we got to the Butcher Shop she hollered at me, 'Mom!' I hollered, 'What!' She hollered, 'Can you have a baby without being married?' So much for the Big Talk, when you are supposed to hang up the dish towel, invite your daughter to sit at the kitchen table and there present the answers to that most personal question in a non-personal, non-emotional manner. I hollered up, 'It's physically possible but not the right thing to do.' And then the corner and cars interrupted, and I never did finish!" I told her maybe she finished just right. With Jack, she had been warned that boys, by age 10, better "be told everything or there'd be big trouble." When he reached that watershed age, Helen asked, "Anything you want to know?" and he replied, "No." I, of course, never asked him.

I think parenting is an example thing. No matter what advice we might give, it's how we treat each other that children soak up by osmosis. Like when I made camping reservations, and it was dark and rainy when we pulled into Ludington State Park, bone weary, only to be told my reservation was for July 14, not today, July 13. What did Helen say? Did she cry? Rant and rave? No. She laughed. "The Great One has goofed," she said. Elizabeth and Jack, having sneaked aboard a dozen toy creatures by putting them inside the pockets of pillows after I had issued the usual order of no more than two creatures apiece, acted out the tragic scenario using Yacky, Ducky, Finger the Squirrel, et al: "Oh, where will we stay? Don't worry, Ducky, Dad knows a cave in the woods that the bears used to use." That took the edge off my embarrassment, and I did find another campsite for the night. I didn't even scold them for bending my rule. Actually, I only made the rule because a creature fell out of the back seat every time they opened a door.

Remembering stuff like that makes me think that Helen and I, just by being there and being grownups, were teaching about sexuality. The mechanics, as Daisy Mae and Li'l Abner verified, do come naturally if there is love. I admit that we came from small towns where it was shameful to see in the newspaper the name of someone you knew who had been caught speeding, drunk, or guilty of tax evasion. The newspapers were a good source to quote bad examples when we were children. Helen used them too as part of her mothering technique: "Imagine! Ralph Whatshisname receiving stolen property! His mother must be heartbroken!" Elizabeth and Jack would hear this and stop play for a moment. They'd see the distress on our faces and unconsciously resolve that they'd never bring disgrace on their parents by having their names in the papers for having done something bad.

And, of course, this was all part of the quality/quantity time we spent together. The rise of women's lib and the running of women to the workplace, led to the defensive idea that quality time is just as good as quantity time. We know children need both times as much as humanly possible. Someone who loves them must *be* with the children, not popping in and out. For instance, kids should see how their idols (all parents are idols to kids, even bad parents) handle a headache, or fear of spiders, or too many clothes to wash, or anger, or great happiness—all the big and little ups and downs of life. I guess today one can't read from the papers to help guide children—"Man kills 18 people, buries body parts in yard; carjacker kills young woman." It would be like reading a gory novel to your family. Elizabeth once asked Helen, "Mom, are there more good people or bad people in the world?" Helen says she found herself pausing before answering, but she recovered hopefully before the delay was noticed and replied, "Oh, good people! We just don't hear about them." We hope that was true. We hope it's still true.

But now, finally, spring had come. I'd had my eye on "Bluegill II" for more than a year. It had a divided bench which made a nice aisle to walk back and forth from motor to anchor, and I thought a 15 hp Johnson would be about right for all the inland lakes we've got. Helen's verbal shove took me right to it, but I had to wait several weeks for the slush and mush to disappear.

Finally, it was time to try out Bluegill II and see if she'd float. I chose the first warmish day to try her out on Sanford Lake. I forgot it was The First Warmish Sunday Of The Season. I paid the $3 park fee and then I saw the line: boat trailers filled the parking lot and wound around the entry. Big boats, little boats, old "Vacation Daze" next to new "Pequod II," beat-up no-namers on rusty, homemade trailers, next to a sleek racer named "Wet Dream." I watched as each boatman whipped his truck up, and backed in the trailer. The boat slid off, a helper caught its rope, the truck whipped up the ramp and parked the empty trailer across the road in the Trailers Only area. After one and a half hours of studying their style and drinking orange pop, I had my turn.

I whipped the truck around and after backing, suddenly saw the trailer sticking out at a 90 degree angle. I pulled forward, wishing I had practiced somewhere secluded, wishing I didn't have a neck so stiff that I had to use the mirrors, and backed, slower this time … Damn! There was the trailer sticking out the other side. I pulled forward, and some helpful guy came over and gave me strange hand signals that I managed to ignore. Finally I felt the truck dip down. The guy motioned more, so I backed more, set the brakes, hopped out to release the boat while getting wet to my knees, and it floated obediently. I tied it to the dock, got back in the truck and started to pull out the trailer when the guy hailed me from the dock and yelled, "The plug's out! The plug's out!" Luckily, I was still pretty much in a straight line, so I backed up slowly, hauled the boat up far enough to drain out the water, put the plug in, and then slowly launched again while everyone was standing around watching and talking quietly. They had, I suspected, gone through this mortification themselves, a lot like zinging a golf ball off the first tee to the women's tee with fifteen guys watching. At last Bluegill II purred out, and I opened her up. She planed beautifully.

Back home, I pulled up parallel to the curb. Helen came over with a big smile and asked, "Well?"

I said, "It's a good boat."

She said, "I'm happy to hear Bluegill II received your highest praise."

"I only said it's a good boat."

"But that is your highest praise," Helen insisted. "When you said 'Good dog' to Patch he'd wag himself sideways with joy. And 'Good boy' and 'Good girl' made Jack and Elizabeth glow. And when you saw the Tigers play and said 'It was a good game,' I knew that Trammell and Whitaker had a couple double plays, and Gibson hit a home run, and that the Tigers won by two in the ninth."

"And when I say, 'She's a good woman'?"

"Then I know you're talking about your mother! But, honestly, you remember Sue and Jim who had just met the parents of their daughter's husband, and they said, 'They are wonderful people! Just wonderful!"

I said, "I remember. And you asked what that meant. What do wonderful people do to get that description? And you answered yourself with, 'They probably smiled a lot and praised Sue and Jim to high heaven, served filet mignon and never pointed out the shelves of trophies and plaques for sports and community service. The mother wore matching shoes and nylons, and the father reconditioned 1920s cars and …' See? I remember every jealous word."

"Stop it, Hank. You know I wasn't jealous. They're probably divorced by now."

"Jim and Sue?"

"No. The wonderful parents."

I said, "Is this women's intuition?"

"No. Gushers tend to be fakers. We'd never be called 'wonderful' by anyone."

"We probably aren't."

"So there you have it. 'Good' is your highest praise and has to be earned. And I'm proud to remind you that you always say my pies are good, and I made an apple to celebrate."

"They are. And so's the boat."

"Good. When are we going fishing?" Helen asked, not expecting an answer.

She'll find out about my wonderful backing skills soon enough.

Berry season took care of the summer, what with the weeding, the broadcasting of fertilizer and the mowing between 21 rows, gathering over 300 cut-off boxes from our neighborhood Airport Grocery. Seventy-five years ago there was a small airport on that site, just as a metal junk yard cluttered what is now "Junk Yard Tavern," which makes Helen wonder what visitors to town think about those names. There's the buying and hauling of 500 more wooden quart boxes from a wholesaler four hours' drive from town, the repainting and repairing of signs and row markers, the affixing of the large banner across the barn, getting change from the bank, recording the "Open" and "Closed" taped messages, sprucing up the flower garden near the cashier's table, hauling the bench from the basement, and, in between, canning tomatoes and peaches, freezing corn and beans.

Pickers came from September 6 to October 10. No early frost. A typical, confusing season. Some days we had more cars than we had spaces for. Other days I worked on fixing the barn door while Helen watched over six or seven pickers, checked the progress of the popcorn, cut bittersweet and walked back and forth. She found a two-year-old plum tree totally broken into shredded strips by a deer that used it to remove his velvet. A whole forest full of trees, and the deer choose our new, flexible saplings for their annual necessity.

One day an older woman stayed out in the berry field during a steady rain, while I sat in the truck and waited for her to give up. She persisted until she had five soggy quarts. Then said she had better hurry home to a warm bath before she got pneumonia but that she'd have to wash the berries first.

I said, "But we never wash the berries. There's no spray on them. Besides, they're already washed, ha ha, by the rain."

And she said, "But I want to wash the rain *off*." Well, I hoped she was going to make jam, because she would already have the quarts of mashed fruit.

The next morning three pickers showed up at opening hour: 8:30. "Where is everyone?" they asked, probably wondering if something was not right with the berries.

"Oh, they probably think the berries are still wet," I said, "but it only takes an hour of morning sun to dry them off, and the paths between are grass or weed-covered so they don't turn muddy. They'll be here any minute now," I said. I was just like that lifeguard on the beach waiting for swimmers. Well, that's a commercial. The point of it is the people never come because they're at a Memorial Day sale and he sits there all day saying, 'Any minute now.' At 10:00 we had only six pickers. Helen decided to take some berries to our city's only fancy bakery that makes special German cakes and tarts. I helped her pick 21 half-pints that she would offer at $1.00 per.

She came back in an hour and said she had sold them all! But then she added that the manager had said this had to be a one-shot deal because in two days they had blueberries coming in.

"I'm not sure I want a steady picking job, anyway," I said.

Helen agreed, "Me neither. But at least we know if we get bogged down, there is a way out, and we can charge so much more when we pick them ourselves."

The next afternoon, Helen stopped at that same bakery and bought one raspberry tart for $2.49. It was very pretty with its eight, glazed berries on top. We cut it in half and ate it for dessert that evening.

Berry pickers are interesting people. Aside from their having different ideas of time—we've had phone calls at 11:00 p.m. Fridays; we've had phone calls at 8:30 a.m. Sundays—they have different styles and attitudes about picking berries. One gentleman always picks one quart of berries into his own container, never more than one, and although he returns several times each season, he always complains about the berries being either too far apart, too ripe, not ripe enough, or whatever he can think of for that day. One woman phones and phones before the season and comes to pick two times per week. She always picks at least five quarts which are full of yellow berries, overripe berries, and twigs. It hurts us to see it, but it would embarrass her if we started sorting what she's so happily picked. Some people shoot down a row in 20 minutes and ask to be put on a new row and they shoot down that one too. After they've driven away we can usually put another customer on the just-picked rows who will inevitably pick eight quarts and exclaim how many berries there are this year. Each season there are people who say, "I owe you for the ten quarts we picked one afternoon when you were closed. Our children were along and wanted to pick, so I told them we'd pay you later and that you wouldn't mind." We shudder to think how lawyers might handle the case if someone fell into the ditch and broke an ankle while they were trespassing, and we wonder what kind of example trespassing is for the children. We don't care about the 10 quarts.

Helen gets upset by criticism of the crop even if it's all Mother Nature's doing. If the berries "aren't as sweet as last year," I have to remind Helen that other people raved to me that the berries were "sweeter than last year." She says the customers prefer me to her because I give them a few squash or apples or get a chair from the barn. She points out, "The green bench is for sitting." When people measure their own berries by pouring them overflowing into the boxes while saying "My row wasn't too good," Helen wants to shout, "For heaven's sake! Fair is fair!" Funny. She was supposed to be the salesman, and I was supposed to be just the field hand. Maybe teachers are more used to discipline; in my job, the squeaky wheel was just another one of many squeaky wheels that I listened to between tending to the really broken wheels. The study of behaviors would probably give some high school senior good case studies for a paper, if students are still assigned papers, which I doubt now that computers and the internet can call them up so easily. At least we can honestly say that each customer brought along his own idiosyncrasies and personality to enliven our days, and we appreciated each one. At least, I did.

Nevertheless, after the end of the season it crossed my mind that maybe it was time to plow the whole thing under, and next year we'd have August and September to do whatever we wanted. Helen would surely give a speech about character-building, which two months of a daily schedule of commitment must be good for. And what about all the unhappy people we'd leave without their fun, like that mother with four boys who helped her pick while she had a baby girl in her arms? They all happily sang "Shoulder To The Wheel." Or what about the boys who ran happily after that groundhog, or that older couple who pick 11 quarts and give them all away? Helen reminded me how much I enjoy being out at The Land whether I need to be or not. And I answered that at my age, my character's pretty well built, and retirement is supposed to bring freedom to do what we want when we want to.

At least we had agreed in spring that we would not replace any plants that died off. No more 1,000 plants put in one by one on our knees. The place ran more smoothly the last few years, anyway. People almost stopped phoning in July to ask if we had berries ready. And nobody complained that we had raised our price by 25 cents this year. It was necessary, or else the Feds might wonder why we never make a profit. That's partly true. The Feds assume that anyone who sells anything wants to make a profit, so they set up taxes with that in mind. We were more concerned that we were undercutting the market, since an ad had appeared in the local paper under Farm Produce: "Raspberries, U-Pick, $1.75 per pint." We knew that price was okay for Boston or Chicago, but we also knew our conservative customers would pick one pint at that price instead of the average six quarts they pick at our price.

This new competition was 10 miles farther from town than we were and they sold most of their produce to wholesalers. We figured that by the time we decide to quit, our competition will be there, ready and waiting. So, good: we'll raise our price a bit, and they will have to lower theirs in order to compete. In that way we'll be preparing our customers for the future. "Supply and demand" sounds logical, but it rarely operates without some manipulation. Diamonds, for instance, have been in over-abundance for many decades, but since people want them to be "special" and "rare" and "expensive," the owners control the supply. We hope to operate closer to fairness. Market experts have stated that if a price turns away 10% of the buyers, it's the right price. They're probably the same experts who advised the

Grand Hotel on Mackinac Island to charge a fee for people who wanted to stroll along their World's Largest Porch, because there were so many people strolling that their paying guests had to zigzag to get inside. When the Hotel charged a fee, more people came to stroll. We amateurs should be nervous?

Thus endeth berry season for another year. I bet that if I came home one day and said, "I'm going to plow the whole batch under," Helen would say that she was thinking about suggesting it, since we both weren't truly enjoying it like we used to.

The end of October or early November usually means we're free to travel somewhere, celebrate, but I had fishing on my mind. I said to Steve, "Steelhead?" So we loaded the truck camper and pulled the boat to Ludington for some real, intensive fishing on our favorite inland lake. It was lucky Steve was along, because with the camper on, I couldn't see a thing behind me, not even the bicycle flag I had attached to the back end of the boat. We spent three cold days of no-luck fishing and two cold nights of no-heat sleeping.

We've had worse, like back in the 1950s when our roommate Marshall shot a hole in the boat while duck hunting at dawn. And there were those years of Opening Day Trout Fishing when we slept in tents and had to break the ice in the wash bucket.

We've had false starts. Once at 5:30 a.m., four of us piled with our gear into the lemon of all lemons, my 1957 Plymouth, and it was a no go. So we piled our gear into Marshall's 57 Plymouth and by 7:00, managed, in a low-slung way, to get ourselves to our hunting grounds and back home. Then we had two dead 57 Plymouths in the driveway. We left them there until we had slept off "the hunt."

We've had false returns: taking back roads at 10 p.m. with only running lights. We've had false middles: car engine failure that one of us volunteered to get fixed while the rest of us fished.

Snowstorm

Snow came
swirling in circles, plastering
with careless trowel,
shouting songs of drunken masons
piling drifts of revelry
till dawn.

The volunteer had fallen over a tackle box in the boat, hurt his back, and could barely crawl. But he saved the day and got the car fixed, whereas he never could have sat in a boat. Jack and I have ice-fished in 15 degrees with a 25 mph wind and no shanty. Nothing can stop us guys from having fun.

Helen has had her share of fun, too. I remember especially that day in March when we decided it was time to try some of that spring skiing that everyone raves about: light jackets, sunshine, no crowds at the lifts. Elizabeth and Jack had Easter vacation. The sun was shining. We put our downhill skis, poles, and boots, in the aisle of the camper and planned to lean the skis and poles against a tree once we got to our site, thus making room for us to get inside. Boyne Mountain being about a three-hour drive north, it would still have snow even though our town had its yearly black slush.

We had a lovely, sunny drive and parked at a campground about five miles from the resort. We settled down, anticipating a cozy evening and an early start for the hills. The camper shuddered. We zipped an opening in the canvas side and saw a wonderful snowfall beginning. Perfect, we thought, 34 degrees and new spring snow. But then the winds picked up more, and we realized we had a real snowstorm out there. The thermometer dipped to 20, then to 10. Our longjohns, boots, heavy sweaters (in Michigan, we don't leave home without them) and electric heater worked hard just to keep us warm enough to be able to hold our books with one hand while keeping the other in our pockets.

Then Helen said, "I'll boil Easter eggs for tomorrow's breakfast. That will add warmth to the place, too." So she boiled eggs, adding onion skins to color them a festive brown. That done, we gave up trying to stay warm and crawled into our sleeping bags, shuddering the night away. The thermometer had registered zero the last time I checked.

I woke at 7:00 and glanced around the camper, sensing

something was different. The heater was correctly silent; I always turn if off at night as a precaution. A brightness flooded the place. My breath looked like heavy smoke. And then I saw the icicles—tiny, half-inch icicles covering all the canvas over our beds and across the sides of the camper like a miniature stalactite show in our own little cave. Helen's Easter fun decorated more than eggs.

Helen snuggled close to me. "I'm freezing!" she said.

"I'll get the heater going," I said. I jumped gingerly out of the sleeping bag.

"What's all that sparkly stuff?" Helen asked.

Elizabeth and Jack woke and said, "Wow!" They dressed quickly and began knocking off the icicles. I gave them paper towels, not wanting a flood when they melted. We finally were able to unzip the windows: three feet of blazingly white snow! Helen and Elizabeth trudged through the over-the-knee mounds to get to the heated bathrooms, and they didn't return until I had the toast, bacon, and hard-boiled eggs set out. After breakfast I used our folding camp shovel to try to clear out the snow in front of the truck, knowing it was hopeless. We were snowbound for the day, a long day.

We made it to the slopes the next day, but didn't warm up until we were home. Helen said, "At least you didn't make it rain." So much for spring skiing.

Helen's fun also included trying to prepare spaghetti from scratch on the Coleman stove atop Lake Michigan dunes, the blowing sand sputtering the flame. Remembering that, she asked, "Why didn't I use the canned sauce? How could I be so stupid!" I reminded her that there was no such thing then, and she said, "Oh. I forgot. McDonald's hadn't even sold a million hamburgers yet. And noodles were plain noodles before pasta became green. You know, lately I need an interpreter for recipes.

What do you think 'haricots verts' is? or 'radicchio'? Remember when a vet from WWII would say he dreamed of returning home to Mom's roast beef and mashed potatoes with gravy? And a Vietnam War vet said he missed McDonald's. Desert Storm was so short the vets didn't have time to miss dinners but probably longed for their cappuccino."

It's computers, I guess, that are the cause of our lives being changed so quickly. I do admire this next generation's ease with computers, but I just hope they aren't trusting them too much. I mean, you still have to be able to recognize situations that just don't make sense, like in the banking end of it. The computer says our bill payment is one number, and I say it is another. Lo and behold, I am right. No one else had spotted the fact that the computer's numbers *didn't make sense*. Computers also aid all the experts so they can spew out information faster than ever before. Now third graders get all this information about global warming, ozone depletion, loss of species, and destruction of the environment until they think the globe has been totally ruined. They aren't told that there are many different "experts" and many different conclusions.

Computers may be taking over the job of "gods" from the TV. Helen's golfing partner in the spring league said that her granddaughter gets hysterical if she live-traps a squirrel that has been chewing on her garage. Judgment, balance, and testing have to check all this easy computer information; otherwise, it all will be just another chapter in the "butter is bad for you, oops, it's okay for you, oops, it's eggs that are bad, oops, they are good, oops, it's coffee that's bad" and on and on. Computers, wonderful aids that they are, do sometimes get ahead of the human brain and really louse things up. But thankfully it's the next generation that's going to have to watch out and be diligent. I only have to catch a stray error now and then.

Fishing season was over, and the lull before the Christmas rush was upon us. Helen usually rids herself of profundities during these slow times.

"Did you know that Audubon ate bald eagles?"

I was caught off guard as usual, being deep into the last chapter of some mystery.

"What?"

"Audubon ate bald eagles."

"Who said?"

Helen answered, "I read it somewhere. There were so many then."

"What did they taste like?"

"They didn't say. You're the one who eats pats and quail or grouse or bobwhites or whatever."

"Same thing, Helly. I keep telling you, quail and bobwhites are essentially the same birds."

"Well, they didn't say."

"Probably like chicken," I said. "Anything strange like snakes and Cambodian monkeys always tastes like chicken, as if chicken were delicious. How come nothing ever tastes like filet mignon? Then, I might want to try it."

"Oh, finish your book."

I turned back a page to figure out what I'd read. Before I figured it out, Helen had another thought to share.

"Tomorrow I want to call the City Parks to change that **ATTENDENT** sign before the fast pitch tournament and all those out-of-towners see it."

"Nobody would notice."

"It's embarrassing. And what about the Great Poetry Revival they're talking about? You know what?"

"What."

"It's inner spillings all over again! Just like the 1960s. A guy in Detroit stood on a table and recited his so-called poem, naked. If that's revival, I say leave it dead. And another thing: you know my thing about apostrophes?"

"I..t..apostrophe..s means it is or it has," I correctly responded.

"Yes, but there's another one. The most highly respected writers use it, and it's accepted and called double possessive."

"Like what? I need an example."

"They write, *a friend of my mother's* with an apostrophe."

"That's wrong?"

"Here. Read this," Helen said.

I read: *McKensey had been a great friend of both Vince Smith's and my father's.*

"Why did I spend all those years teaching 'the tail of the dog, the dog's tail' if *this* is what's okay? What am I not understanding? What's going on?"

I said, "Helly, we ought to decide about going to Florida."

"What brought that on?"

"I don't know. Maybe your crack about being seventy."

"Seventy?"

"You know, the other day when you said we won't do in our seventies what we don't do in our sixties." I thought that explained it.

"Good grief. That was months ago. You didn't say anything. I never know what the heck you're thinking," Helen said.

Probably true. I had warned Helen on the way to getting our marriage license that I tend to be quiet. I remember she was wearing a pretty pink dress and said, "I'll talk enough for both of us." The courthouse was closed. We tried again the next day. I don't remember what she wore or what we said, but we got our license. Helen realized that not talking much doesn't mean not thinking much, and sooner or later we manage to straighten out our misunderstandings. So after I mentioned Florida, we tossed out sporadic ideas over the next few days and decided to leave

… that is the Question

Would you kill yourself again
to know what you know?
If I said I loved you, then
would you kill yourself? Again
go in secret where you've been?
Should it scare me so
if you would kill yourself again
to know what you know?

mid-February, go to our favorite Grand Outdoors camping spot, and stay long enough to decide if it was time to buy our own pad.

The Grand Outdoors was really a retirement community with all the amenities and activities of a small town. But we weren't ready to acknowledge that it wasn't camping, that we might actually be ready to become the true retirees that outsiders call "duffers." We would take our truck/camper that had no TV, no air conditioner, no microwave, and no electric coffee pot. We had no reason not to stay six or eight weeks if we wanted to. Helen added the depressing observation that now that Jack had bought his own house in Colorado, both our children were totally adults, completely and thoroughly. Even though Elizabeth had had their dreamhouse-under-remodeling for almost ten years now, it wasn't until Jack bought his house that we heard the sharp clank of the other shoe dropping, loud enough to be a cowboy boot, spurs and all.

And, as Helen's mood usually popped up in her poetry, I could have panicked over the last one she had placed on my table. It was the most depressing thing I've ever read. It starts, "Would you kill yourself again / To know what you know?" and it gets worse.

"Where do you get such morbid ideas?" I asked, almost afraid of the answer.

"But, look! It got a tie for third place, and it's the first triolet I've ever tried! It's very restricted, what with all the repetitions and the rhyme scheme, but once you learn what the rules are, you're allowed to bend them to make it a modern triolet."

"It's depressing."

"Well, you don't think about things like dying."

"Can't do anything about it."

"I can't understand how anyone with any sense and view of his place on the planet and knowledge of all the attempts of religion to ease mortals' minds—I don't understand how anyone can *not* think about it."

"It's easier just to leave it up to that Good God you always talk about."

"I'm still trying to figure out if I can trust Him."

"You've got a choice?"

"Well, if He's just playing games like some philosophers say, I think He'd like some of us to try to call His bluff and He'd get a good laugh at our attempts and enjoy us more than those who just sit there without a thought in their heads," Helen said. Somewhat defensively, I thought.

I said, "And if He's not playing games?"

"Well, then Something is. Just look at the fish in the depths of the oceans and all the bizarre stuff they do."

"It's not bizarre to the fish."

"At least reading that poem made you think, didn't it? It is just a poem. I'm very happy with it. It won a prize! You should congratulate me, not cross-examine me!"

Maybe I did over-react. She certainly acted happy about it. It's that creative mind confusing me again I suppose. But that night, out of the blue, she sighed, "Our chickens have run under the fence."

"Hey, at least we know where they ran to," I said. "Let's go visit Jack. Having family visit a new house helps turn it into a real home." I was beginning to echo some of Helen's wisdoms. A little light from Venus, I suppose.

We made a quick Friday-Monday visit to Colorado Springs. Enough for the grand tour of the house, the city, and the surrounding scenery all nestled very close to the Rockies. We couldn't find a thing to criticize or to warn Jack about. In fact, we were both thrilled, and proud. His house is on a cul-de-sac, one of three deadends that cut sideways up a hill, so the view from his porch is magnificent with the mountains west and the city and Kansas, east. The streets and towns have the flavor of Spain, The West, yuccas, antelope, and sky instead of the Beltway's British names, cherry trees, and crowds. We were glad we would now be able to envision him living in his own house after all those years of different apartments, many that we didn't get a chance to visit.

Helen philosophized, "Now I know why the Indians had sacred mountains. Pikes Peak made my neck prickle. Wherever we went, I'd look up and there he was, watching." I had just thought the grandeur was refreshing, but then, I'm no poet. She went on, "What do you think 'gut-feeling' really is?" Used to these musings/questions that have no early warning system, I said, "Gut-feeling is what we feel when we make the right decisions."

Helen said, "Then what about, 'Let your conscience be your guide?"

"What about it?"

"Well, which do you listen to when you have to make a decision?"

I said, "My guts. I have no conscience."

"Be serious!"

"Okay. It's still my gut. Now what's this all about?"

"Well, when Jack wondered if he should buy the house or not, I said, 'Go with your gut feeling.' "

"What's wrong with that? If he made a mistake, he can always sell it," I said.

"But I didn't tell him to pray over it."

"Thinking, wishing, hoping, listening, hesitating—what's the difference?"

Helen rested her knitting on her lap, looked at my benign (I'm sure) face, and said, "I think that's how angels talk to us."

"Through our **guts**?"

"No, our 'gut.' Our inner depth. Why not? Is that an embarrassment to angels? Is spongy gray matter any less an embarrassment? I think the Bible's 'be still' meant that when you know in your gut what's right, do it. And then a person sat and pondered, got up, and did it, and then said that an angel told him to do it. Then his friends were astonished and asked the person to describe how it *felt* and he said 'airy and pleasant and secure like a mother's love.' So people drew airy, winged, pretty, pictures from the description. What do you think?"

"I'll need some time on that one. First tell me where the conscience went."

"The people just changed a physical and emotional feeling into a mental state—the conscience—so that 'gut feeling' got elevated and given a nice name. First it happens in the gut."

"I'll think about it," I said.

Of course I tried to forget about it. What thoughts! Guts, or rather, gut, and angels! Making decisions, though, became easier if I thought about my gut feelings as sincere messages from angels.

And, of course, I had that gut feeling about the amber, not that angels care about amber.

Tuesday was a crisp, sunny day—the kind Michigan offers in early winter when we start hoping for snow. I went into the barn through the side door as usual to get the saw and haul a few more logs out of the woods. Whenever I open the side door I have to be prepared for anything. Usually a black snake slides out between my feet, and sometimes mice do the same. Today, nothing moved, but a strong breeze hit my face. The barn is usually quite warm even under a weak sun. The window was open? The window I had nailed shut and put screens across after someone had thrown a melon through the one upstairs? I went around the boat to get a closer look and there it was. The glass had been removed. And I hadn't had to step around the rototiller. It wasn't there. Neither was the shovel, the shiny fat chain, the scythe, or a few other tools. The tractor and all the big stuff were there. I went outside to see if Woody was still there. He was.

Helen evidently heard the truck in the driveway because she met me outside with the unspoken question of why I was back so soon.

"We've been robbed." I said.

"The trailer!"

"No. They broke into the barn."

"The boat!"

"No. A bunch of little stuff and the rototiller. They came in through the window and opened the big door."

"Why not the boat, then?"

"Probably because they didn't have a flat bed, or time. Just grabbed that nice shiny chain I just bought. And lots of tools, a shovel. But Woody wasn't touched," I said.

"Why in the world would anyone want Woody!" Helen said, bewildered.

Uh-oh.

"Well, ah, I suppose, ah, well why would anyone want a shovel? I gotta call the sheriff. Got the number somewhere?" I said.

Insurance covered our losses. Like most victims, we rationalized by being grateful that the B&E wasn't into our home, or worse, our home while we were there asleep. We could name at least six couples whose homes had been either broken into or trashed. It was disgusting. The sheriff said our stuff was long gone, sold for drug money. They were probably not pros, just punks.

G. B. Shaw had said that cocaine use grew in the 1920s as a release for "after the war." He didn't say crime rose dramatically, though, so I think the users had their own money and chose to spend it on cocaine, opium, or laudanum, as artists have been forever known to do to ease their frustrations. Of course, the drugs were not as pure as now and tended to put them to sleep rather than to make them violent, but violence did not seem to go hand in glove with drug use until people without money decided they also would choose drugs "for release." At the beginning of this chain reaction was my barn. For months afterward, I'd reach for something in the barn only to realize it was among the missing. It didn't amount to enough money to make a fuss, but it was darn annoying. And it was scary. We hoped it was a one-shot deal. When we told Elizabeth she said, "So where were all those nosy neighbors who reported Brad's car parked in front of the barn when we were in high school!"

Well, Christmas would take our minds off of everything else for awhile. This year Elizabeth and family would be coming to our house, as would Jack—a wonderful reunion for us all, a chance for Jack to catch up on his nieces and nephews. Actually, Helen and I always feel as if we're playing catch-up, too. Grandchildren are always cuddly new babies to us. Each visit they have grown up into something different—little girls and little boys and then, suddenly, into pre-teens, each stage bringing new views that they have, new talents they discovered, new excitements, new challenges. We try hard to keep up. Christmas, especially, has an added aura of warmth, love, and expectation shining a bit brighter: the star effect, probably.

I don't remember my childhood Christmases. Helen asked if I had presents on Christmas Eve or on Christmas Day. I only remember going to church and having Bible verses to memorize. I must have gotten, maybe, some clothes, which would have been better than the usual second-hand overalls I always wore. But we weren't any poorer than my friends, and I don't remember being unhappy or ever desperately wanting any special thing, unlike that boy and his BB gun that's on TV every year. We had a basketball, and our gang played our version of roundball in our driveway all the time, even in winter. I always managed to find some kind of job that paid just enough to get me to the movies and, later, through college. I guess I never did anything expensive.

In the 1940s, we could still hitchhike in relative safety. Once Joe and I did get picked up by drunks. We escaped when they stopped at a gas station. But we didn't think we were ever in danger of being shot for our shoes. We managed to get from Michigan to Florida and back with 20 cents left over.

But Christmas? We did always have a tree and there was always a feeling of festivity. If my folks wished for more, I never noticed. Helen's Christmases had all the magic that a little girl could hope for, especially a little girl with a lot of imagination. She said her home town had a main street five blocks long, and red and green lights hung across it from every telephone pole all the way from the Catholic church on the hill to the woolen mills. It was a game to count how many were burned out, as there always were some. She listened to Santa's progress as reported by Billie the Brownie on WTMJ. And she helped her mother bake and bake and bake, especially the 12 inch gingerbread men and the 1-1/2 inch gingerbread boys, which they decorated by dipping toothpicks into frosting and shaping hats, mittens, suspenders, whatever creative fancy struck them. Helen still does it the same way today. As she says, that ritual assures Santa's arrival, and I suspect it really does.

It was the end of October, so Helen began laying her groundwork for Christmas.

"Can you think what to give Jack?"

"Give?" I asked.

"For Christmas!"

"It's two months away."

"We might have to order something," Helen said, persisting with her mission.

"UPS takes two days."

"Not if the item's gone."

"Well," I said, "I can't think of anything."

"Hank, you don't try. You wait until about five days before and then you run out and get me whatever's available."

"Not when you have the clerk put it aside with your name on it. Then I go the day before."

"Not funny. And I'm not going to do that anymore. I'm gonna make you work. In fact, one year you surprised me with short, red skis, and one year with a pearl from Hong Kong. And an opal from Australia another time. You were working and traveling then, so it was quite a while ago. But you don't do too badly when backed into a corner."

"Four out of 38 ain't bad."

"Oh, you probably got about 20. Santa Claus should seem more real to you than he does to our grandchildren, the way the decorations, gifts, cookies, sweet rolls and everything all magically appear."

"Well, you're good at it."

"And, of course, you didn't have time, being at work until 6:00."

"Actually," I confessed, "I don't think coming home at 3:00 would have inspired me to bake cookies."

"How did I ever manage? And playing Scrabble with Mom every night, besides."

"You were young. Heck, when Elizabeth was eighteen months old, we moved into this house ten days before Christmas, and you were three months pregnant and we invited my sister to come."

"Crazy. Well, those crazy times are over and I think this year we should cut back on everything. One gift apiece. Or maybe two. Of course, there has to be a book for Jack and some clothes for Elizabeth because that's always been the main thing about their Christmases all these years . You know Gordon says there's no Santa?'

"He's old enough."

"At least he had a taste of the magic for awhile."

"You mean like the lying?"

"Cut it out, Hank. You know what I mean. Experts say only adults think of the illogicalness of the chimney and going to every house in one night. Children love make-believe and they learn from it all the time. They pour invisible tea, make airplanes out of legos. But then we teach kids not to trust their gut, so they lose their wonder, their belief in things unseen that the *Wizard of Oz* was all about: courage, hope, love, common brain sense. It's funny, you know: parents take their children to Disney World but then tell them that Santa is a lie. Forcing reality on children who are too young to accept it causes them to hate reality later. Santa gives the equivalent of the ancient feeling of 'bliss.' Santa gives an emotional warmth that can last a lifetime. Young children have to grow into intellectual reality at their own pace."

"Maybe there's more serious stuff to learn these days. Take poli-sci majors. Countries change names and politics every six weeks. And take electrical engineers, doctors, scientists—computers are old before they even leave the plant; more uses for lasers and other star wars' machines are found every day; new medicines, new galaxies even!"

"But one person doesn't have to know it all. And, besides, I'm talking about what's *missing*. Kids know when their text books have been 'dummied down.' Authors throw up their hands, and their lunch, when told 'chocolate cookies' must not be used in their books. Librarians have to fight to keep classics on the shelves. These older students want the truth and they know when it's being circumvented. They want to be inventive and learn what's important and ethical and decent and wise. Kids know when self-esteem and diplomas are fake rewards.

Vandalism, I think, is caused by kids who know they were gypped; what *they earn*, they would respect."

"Sounds like you're promoting those courses called Life that we used to say were pure Mickey Mouse," I said.

"No. When 'learning for the love of it' is replaced with nothing, when statesmen fall below the level of politicians, when parents are immature, and think 'Participate in your child's education' means 'Interfere with the teacher and principal in order to get your child preferential treatment' so that a pregnant eighth grader spends math class telling her male peers how 'the baby is kicking all the time'—then it's time to answer that question asked in the early 1970s, 'It's 11 p.m. Do you know where your children are?' with 'What children? There aren't any children anymore!' When TV says it is only reflecting the immorality and violence that already exists in society, then educators and parents should tell them that they have chosen only one part of society to reflect and have lied to us by claiming it is all of society. Besides, TV by its nature does not lead to any kind of truth about anything, because nothing on TV is real. For starters, nobody has such white teeth or clear skin. And even on nature shows, the long range lens is so far away that the sound of the animal walking in tall grass is made by a guy crunching papers and breaking celery in the editing room. And if you're thrilled to hear a proud eagle's commanding scream, you are most likely hearing the scream of a red-tailed hawk. An eagle's 'scream' is a submissive-sounding whistle. The hawk's cry is dubbed in. And backgrounds are generally fakes. Jack and I once saw a movie on TV in which the people all obeyed their ruler, who spoke to them weekly via monitors. Trouble was he'd been dead for ten years. And even documentaries often distort truth by such subtle means as playing background doomsday music when reporting on facts that do not match the music. Remember Dr. Feynman's admonition to test the premise, or else generations learn from a 100-year-old false premise that no one bothered to test?"

"I thought we were talking about Christmas, Helly."

"Well, I get carried off, and you just let me ramble and don't add any words of wisdom."

"While you were off, I did get an idea. Jack could use a British type of book with some humor instead of those tomes you always give."

"He's interested in tomes. He's interested in everything. He reads your dumb mysteries, too."

I said, "Well, that's my word of wisdom."

"Why don't you find something, then?"

"You're in charge of books."

"Maybe we should just have food and hugs this year. That's really all we need."

"And a tree," I added.

"Of course a tree! Maybe one gift apiece. I really wish you'd help. Like that year I thought I had already spent too much and you went out and got a Ping-Pong table."

"I just thought it'd be fun."

"It is. You think bigger stuff than I do. So why don't you help?"

"You do just fine," I said, hoping I escaped the lasso again.

Santa gave us another Christmas to savor. Abbey politely handed out presents after Ben read the names tags to her. Year-old Lorri happily played on the floor with the ribbons and bows, everyone smiled, laughed, glowed, ate candy, cookies, and butterhorns. How lucky we were. Hard hard we try to keep being lucky.

Helen didn't phone Hannah or Nick; they didn't phone either. Brief notes on cards said all were in their usual places, so phone calls just didn't happen. But I knew Helen was getting antsy about that custom, now that we were all getting close to that dangerous age when any old ache could mean something

Message To Our Children

Christmas begins when you come.
The tree will stay bright and expectant
and all we had no time to do, will be done,
for Christmas begins with The Coming
the coming of a child
eager in hope, resplendent
in love, full-strength
and new to this Earth
when the days were all green, and gaiety
circled around the dark eye of time.

Gingerbread boys have been frosted with care,
crepe paper chains reglued.
The angel in pink is poised near the star,
plaster lambs encircle the creche
and the tin bugle is ready to sound.

All wait,
suspended,
as if now were then.
All wait
for you to bring Christmas again.

bad. Yet Helen, being an external optimist with internal doubts, went cheerfully on to our next self-imposed challenge: buying a pad in Florida. First, though we'd have to survive January.

January gave only enough snow for four X-C ski outings, one with our grand and goofy potluck group (during which there was much falling down and teasing, "Who designated this route as intermediate, anyhow? George? You black-diamond downhiller?") followed by Steve's pepper chili fit for only his cast iron intestines, followed by naps for the guys and quiet talk by the women. Helen later said that Sylvia, still being a dedicated teacher, told endearing stories about her kindergartners. Ann observed that "being with men who ski/nap, golf/nap, cut the grass/nap, is like living with babies in the house again!" which had brought knowing nods. Alas, the poor lassies were deprived of knowing the benefits of a good snore.

Sub-zero cold then descended upon Michigan, which always means less snow and more ice. Neither suited the truck/camper's heating equipment, so on February 12 we loaded up the truck and headed south for six weeks in the sunshine.

Outside Nashville some rain showed up on the windshield, and the outside thermometer registered 34. Helen hates icy driving. I don't relish it, but it's better with the camper than with the trailer slipping along behind. "Let's ask a trucker what's happening," Helen urged, actually saying it as a voice command.

So I called "Breaker, breaker. Northbound anyone? How are the roads south of Nashville?"

Back came the clear voice of a trucker: "Hello southbound. It's treacherous. Get off while you can." He talked regular English, having recognized my call as coming from a regular person, whereas to another trucker he would have talked Big Rig Lingo that Helen and I couldn't interpret.

I answered, "Preciate it," which probably made a few truckers smile.

We drove off on the first exit and drove slowly to the first hotel just as the rain turned to ice. The parking lot was already a glazed black. The hotel turned out to be the huge complex of the Grand Ole Opry. We figured we could afford one night's stay in this emergency. When I registered, talk was about "severe ice storm" so I signed up for two nights much to Helen's relief and delight. At breakfast we heard that the hotel was using its auxiliary power, and all of Nashville and south was in gridlock.

So we had our own paradise. We went to dinner, saw the Grand Ole Opry radio show, which was amazingly dull. Should have gone to the TV extravaganza like everyone else did. When we left, the highway was clear and dry, but right up to the white line on the right were hundreds of downed trees with tops cut off at the line. Farther off the highway, trees and roads still glistened. It took four to seven days' work for the crews to restore power. Blessed be all those brave people who rush *into* storms instead of *away* from them. Surely we made their jobs easier by staying out of trouble.

We pulled up to the gate of The Grand Outdoors, all primed to select a cement pad to call our own. The security officer looked us over and politely told us we could not enter. "Not even to drive around and look at lots to buy?" I asked.

"Sorry," he said, "no campers, no motorcycles." We turned around and drove to a campground along the Indian River, took off the camper, and returned to the Grand's gate.

"Okay now?" I asked.

"Go right ahead" he said.

Trucks are a common vehicle in camping communities since

they tow fifth wheels, but even though we didn't have a gun rack in the back window, a camper is symbolic of riffraff, which we surely didn't want in our neck o' the woods. No sirree. We managed to disguise our basic riffraffery quite well as we drove and walked around the sites that were for sale. By the end of the third week, we knew the one with the huge live oak on it had beckoned us. Helen admitted that the live oak might indeed be dying because it looked quite bare of leaves. But she protested that even if it were dead she'd still admire it. And on a brighter notion, she added that maybe live oaks looked like that in February in Florida.

We spent another week looking at oaks, but by then that big tree had become ours in our hearts. We went ahead and became *owners* after 30 years of being transients, or, more nicely put, visitors. Now we had all the same rights and privileges as the owners of the maroon $500,000 RV parked on the maroon, leaf-stenciled driveway under the roof of the $175,000 house. Next year we could bring our 19 foot trailer w/o air, w/o micro, w/o TV, and park it under our big oak tree. We had it made. Happiness is an alligator in the pond on the golf course, a bald eagle nesting a mile from our site, pileated woodpeckers and owls in our palm trees, chuck-will's-widows calling at dusk, tennis, and fishing. Happiness is being retired and having a partner who enthusiastically agrees with my decisions, making them mutually satisfying.

Right under this layer of contentment lurked the berry patch, and near the patch stood Woody. I knew that I'd plow under the plants in April and I knew Helen would agree. What I didn't know was if I could continue to be admonished by the superiority of Woody and his secret every time I went to The Land.

The trip home went fast. We had good weather and felt good about our decisions.

I plowed under the raspberry patch. We had been tending them for twelve years, even though we both knew that a change every five years, whether we really expect one or not, generally gives off renewed energy. If the energy has to be spent fixing a calamity or celebrating something good, it is still change and adjustment that are essential for growth of the spirit.

Helen quickly verified this renewed vigor by announcing, "Did you know that flamingoes get their pink color from eating shrimp?"

"Have you been talking to Nick?"

"Not yet, but that's something I'll have to make a note about to remember to tell him. And listen to this: 'Bacteria extracted from prehistoric bees.' This article says that a scientist has extracted bacteria from the bees embedded for millions of years in amber."

"Sounds like that off-the-wall cold fusion experiment that hadn't been confirmed before the newspapers got it."

"No, no. The guy expects to find new drugs to fight viruses that are now resistant to so many antibiotics."

"Does it say how?"

"It says he wants to extract bacteria from the bees. And he already spent three years testing. And listen to this! His clinic is calling for people to turn in amber for his experiments! Too bad Jube never surfaced. Bet he'd know where some good stuff is. Are you listening? You ought to think about hearing aids."

"I hear you. Let me read the article."

"You think I misread again, don't you? Just because I never fill out questionnaires properly," Helen complained.

"I just want to read it, that's all," I said.

"Well? You're reading and reading. It's a short notice calling for amber just like I told you."

Helen was right. It was a short article. I didn't even see the words. I was seeing **AMBER**. Is the timing right? How should I start?

"Maybe we ought to look in Woody again."

It was calmly said. Just the right touch, I hoped. Helen's eyes said "In Woody? In our Woody? Why? What?" and they grew wide.

It was worse than I thought. I could have used a tirade to gather my thoughts. But I had no reprieve. None. I said, "You know, Helly, when we emptied Woody." She still didn't say anything. "We found those stones."

"They—weren't—you—said—or—you—would have told me."

"Of course I would have done!" (Lord, now I'm talking British!) "I mean if we had found something good, I would have told you. I mean you would have put them in your stone collection or something."

"So what are you saying then?"

"I'm saying maybe we ought to dump Woody and find those funny stones and send them off to the guy since he's asking."

"Again? Dump Woody again?"

"Why not?" I said, calmly. "What have we to lose?"

"Our sanity, for one."

"You like adventure. It'll be fun."

We went out to Woody, and I stood there and looked at him. Helen, I could feel at my neck, was looking more at me than at Woody. Then she said, "You know, he ought to be holding a lyre or something, or have a dog at his feet. He looks so incomplete."

"That's because he always looks like he knows something we don't."

"That's it. That smile." Helen said. "Beats Mona Lisa. You never know about people, do you?"

"People? Woody's a people?"

"People have secrets. I think about that guy with the shy smile who turned out to be a superb concert pianist. And our handsome little neighbor boy who sings big opera. And that downhill acrobat who looks like a hesitant accountant. And there's Dvorak who directed the U. of Wisconsin concert band using an artificial arm that he moved with his back muscles! You just can't figure out people by looking at them, or even living with them. They'll surprise you every time."

Rats. I had hoped to do this without any great philosophizing on good/evil, right/wrong. Helen seemed calm enough, just moved maybe by whatever gets her thought associations going. Maybe it's because it's a nice day,and the raspberries aren't here anymore, and Jube hasn't appeared out of the blue like she'd always hoped, and Hannah and John are unmarried by agreement. Then Helen decided, "Let's do it. You pull, and I'll stand on the edge and lean." We did it. We got out the shiny stones.

"I don't remember these," Helen said.

"Maybe all the tilting and rubbing against the others shines them up," I said.

She accepted the unacceptable, for now, anyway. I was sweating a lot for a coolish June day, but Helen was truly having an adventure. At home, we put the stones on the kitchen table, and Helen tried to fit them together. After turning the pieces around and around, she decided something must be missing. There was almost a shape but not quite a fit. Of course it could have been our own mental crunching, like when somebody sees the devil in ice cubes.

"All those little black specks might be something buggy. Let's call the number and find out if he wants these," Helen suggested.

"Let's not," I said.

"After all our trouble!"

"Let's just mail them, I mean. They say no questions asked

but what's to stop them from snooping around later? Trace the call? See if they're, er, stolen or something?"

"Oh for Pete's sake. Too many mystery books."

"Helly, we don't know how they got in there, do we."

"I'm going to call Hannah and she'll say, 'No lie!' and we'll have a good laugh. Hey, what about Wanda? Should she look inside Wanda, too? My gosh, you don't suppose Jube … ."

"I have no idea about Wanda or Jube or Woody or anything. You can write a cliff-hanger about it and dress it up if you want to, but I'm just going to mail these off with no return address."

"My, my, you're taking all the fun out of this."

I said, "I'm sorry. Go call Hannah if you want. But after I mail these, I'm done with the whole business."

"It—could—upset her. I mean it might just remind her of what she's been trying to forget: Jube. But I must talk to her, Hank. They had so much amber she could donate to science."

"What if she already dumped Wanda and didn't tell *you*?"

"Then I wouldn't know and wouldn't care. But she knows we have Woody, so why would she keep it a secret?"

I wiped off each stone and put them in a tissue-cushioned box. I felt as if, as if I were wrapping a present for a mistress. I weighed the package, put on seven stamps, and dropped it in the box on Main Street, 15 blocks from the drop box on our corner. I almost drove to Saginaw but caught myself from getting too paranoid. Instead, I went to my haven and healer: The Land. I couldn't go straight home. I had to give myself a little time to get a better vantage point about all this silliness.

It had to be silliness, didn't it? Anything else would be absolutely too far-fetched for any Reasonable Man to consider. Would Helen decide to let it rest? Hmmph. I expected that one day when I least expected it, she'd say something like, "Jube stole the amber and hid it there and planned to come back someday and get it, so he made us unknowing accomplices, and probably Wanda has even more."

And I'd say, "With a sledge hammer while we're standing there watching?"

And she'd say, "He could have dinged Wanda like the farm hand, and found the stones like we did and got curious about Woody and …" She could be phoning Hannah right now. But Wanda could just be a decoy. Would Jube be that shrewd? And Pack didn't even notice Woody, so that means he had no clue.

On the other hand, Helen might decide we did a good turn for science. On the other hand, after all these years I've only learned to be prepared for a surprise. Like when she up and went to Lansing to testify on the pro side for a local chemical plant and was the only female speaker. Nothing came of it. She told me that she wished she had thought to wear a house dress, to have her hair in curlers, and to carry a snuffing baby. That would have given headlines and most certainly helped the cause. I'll never really be able to guess her reactions. Of course, when she's ticked off and doesn't talk to me for an evening, she complains that I never even notice. Well, the facts are on my side in this. We don't know the amber is valuable and we don't know how it got there.

I found myself looking at Woody (habit, I guess). He smiled his darn Boy Buddha smile at me. That did it. I wrestled him around until he faced the woods. Now that our berries weren't here, he might as well cast his spell over the fauna of the woods. The squirrels, rabbits, raccoons, woodchucks, snakes, foxes, deer, hawks, and turkey vultures could use his blessing as they ran around trying to eat each other.

Pleased with my trick, I put my hand on the top of Woody's curly head and mustered up a loud voice with great authority: "Look ol' buddy Buddha, you don't intimidate me anymore. I don't have to think about amber ever again. I don't want any of its rewards, and I don't judge Jube for what he might have done.

I'm perfectly happy with the way things are, and I don't want for anything in this world. So you and I are now calling a draw. Don't for a minute think this is some sort of confession, either. I know what I am and I'm perfectly content to be what I am. I'm not a liar; I'm not a keeper of secrets. I am a keeper of *peace* just like you are. Furthermore, I'm a sentient being and you aren't, so you can't be more enlightened than I am!"

That felt good. It was great to relieve myself of all those thoughts, to free myself from his subliminal influence. Now I truly felt renewed, ready to go home and laugh with Helen over all of our machinations, ready to start the new phase of our lives in Florida, ready to come back out here and gather the wood, watch the deer wrecking our trees, the raccoons wrecking our corn, the swallows chasing away the bluebirds. Well, I just felt happy to be part of it all. I turned and took three steps, but then I stopped and looked back at Woody. I think he winked!

During the drive home I remonstrated myself: "What an imagination! You're acting like you're Calvin and Woody is Hobbes!" I pulled into the garage, turned off the ignition, unbuckled my seat belt, and stared at the back wall through the windshield. I saw the lawn chairs hanging near the beams, and next to them the shovel, rakes, and the white wire fencing. On the shelf the birdseed and the concrete mushrooms Helen likes to put in her flowerbeds; and below, the birdbath, the lawn-mower, the bikes I should have wintered in the basement; and above them that old shelf with the hole in it for Jack's basketball and the grooves cut out for the kids' bats they got at a Tiger game. And I just sat there awhile, looking, musing.

Helen rapped on the window.

"What's the matter!"

"Nothing."

"What are you doing sitting there?" she asked.

"Nothing."

"I saw the truck, and you didn't come and didn't come."

I got out, and she put her arm around my waist and hooked her thumb in my belt loop. I said, "I've been thinking." Helen looked up with a flicker of alarm. I said, "I've been thinking that maybe it's time we start looking for that little, white, Ford convertible you've always wanted." Helen emitted an unladylike squeal of delight, and then, gathering all of her charms, said, "And can we look for a computer, too?"

She did a goofy little "Yes!" dance into the house. I quickly followed.

Being old folks might be fun after all.

Some poems were previously published in

Michigan Natural Resources Magazine
PSM: *Golden Song, Convergence*
Prize Poems of National Federation of State Poetry Societies
Frog Gone Review